The Blood of the Fallen

Fairy tales, Folk tales, Legends & Mythology, Volume 8

Patrick William Lee

Published by Starlit Tales Publishing, 2024.

THE BLOOD OF THE FALLEN

First edition. September 3, 2024.

Copyright © 2024 Patrick William Lee.

ISBN: 979-8227016737

Written by Patrick William Lee.

Table of Contents

To the unsung heroes who rise in the face of darkness,

To those who find strength in unity and courage in adversity,

This tale is for you.

And to the fallen—

Your sacrifices are never forgotten.

May your legacy light the path for all who come after.

With deepest gratitude to the warriors of the heart, who fight not just for today, but for the promise of a brighter tomorrow.

Chapter 1: The Prophecy of Blood

The Ancient Words

In the heart of the ancient kingdom of Valdoria, nestled deep within the shadows of the Orinthian Mountains, there existed a temple as old as time itself. Carved from the very rock of the mountains, the Temple of Whispers stood as a testament to the ancients' knowledge and their fear of what was yet to come. It was here, amid the cold stone and flickering torches, that the prophecy was first uttered—a prophecy that would echo through the ages and lay the groundwork for the cataclysmic events that would follow.

The air inside the temple was thick with incense, the sweet and bitter scents mingling with the faint hint of earth and dust. In the center of the temple, a circle of robed figures stood in silent prayer, their hands raised to the heavens. At their feet lay a stone altar, its surface engraved with symbols that only the most learned scholars could decipher. It was here, at this sacred altar, that the prophecy of blood was first revealed.

The High Priestess, an ancient woman with eyes clouded by time and wisdom, stood at the head of the altar. Her voice, though frail, carried the weight of ages as she began to speak the words that would shape the destiny of kingdoms.

"In the days to come," she intoned, "when the stars align and the blood moon rises, a great battle shall be waged. Kingdoms shall fall, and the earth shall be stained with the blood of the fallen. From this blood, a hero shall arise—a child born of tragedy, destined to lead the forces of light against the darkness."

The robed figures remained silent, their heads bowed in reverence as the prophecy continued.

"Beware the signs," the High Priestess warned. "For they shall herald the coming of this battle. The earth shall tremble, and the skies shall darken. The rivers shall run red, and the cries of the dying shall fill the air. And when the blood moon casts its shadow upon the land, the time shall be at hand. The hero shall rise from the ashes of despair, bearing the mark of the fallen, and shall wield the power to change the course of fate."

The High Priestess paused, her eyes closing as if she could see the events unfolding before her.

"But know this," she whispered, her voice barely audible. "The hero's path is fraught with danger, and the line between light and darkness is thin. Should the hero falter, all shall be lost, and the world shall descend into eternal night."

The prophecy was complete. The temple fell into silence, the only sound the crackling of the torches and the faint rustle of robes as the figures slowly dispersed. The words of the prophecy would be passed down through the generations, their meaning debated and studied by scholars and warriors alike. But as the years turned to centuries, the prophecy became more legend than truth, its warnings fading into the mists of time.

Yet, in the darkest corners of the kingdom, there were those who still believed. Those who knew that the prophecy was not mere legend, but a warning—a warning that the time of bloodshed and heroism was drawing near.

The Kingdom of Valdoria

VALDORIA WAS A KINGDOM of great power and even greater secrets. It was a land of towering mountains and vast forests, where the people lived in harmony with the land and its ancient magic. The kingdom was ruled by King Aldric, a wise and just ruler who had led his people through times of peace and prosperity. But even as the kingdom flourished, there were whispers of unrest, of dark forces gathering in the shadows, waiting for the time to strike.

The capital city of Eldoria was a bustling hub of activity, its streets filled with merchants, craftsmen, and travelers from distant lands. The city was a marvel of architecture, with towering spires and grand palaces that reflected the wealth and power of the kingdom. But beneath the surface, there was a sense of unease, a feeling that something was amiss.

In the royal palace, King Aldric sat upon his throne, his brow furrowed in thought. He had heard the whispers, the rumors of the prophecy that spoke of a great battle and a hero born of tragedy. He had read the ancient texts, consulted with his advisors, and even sought the counsel of the temple priests. But no one could say for certain when the prophecy would come to pass, or who the hero would be.

"Your Majesty," a voice called from the entrance of the throne room. Aldric looked up to see his most trusted advisor, Lord Thorne, approaching with a look of concern on his face.

"What is it, Thorne?" Aldric asked, his voice weary.

"There have been reports, sire," Thorne replied. "Strange occurrences in the northern provinces. The earth trembles, and the skies have darkened. The rivers have turned a deep shade of red, and the people are frightened."

Aldric's heart sank. These were the signs foretold in the prophecy, the harbingers of the coming battle.

"Have the scouts reported any enemy activity?" Aldric asked, trying to keep his voice steady.

"None, sire," Thorne replied. "But the people fear that it is only a matter of time. They believe the prophecy is coming to pass."

Aldric stood, his hands gripping the arms of his throne. "We must prepare," he said, his voice resolute. "Send word to the generals. I want our forces ready to defend the kingdom. And send for the temple priests. We need to understand what we are facing."

Thorne bowed and left the throne room to carry out the king's orders. Aldric remained standing, his thoughts racing. The prophecy was no longer just a legend; it was becoming a reality. And if the prophecy was true, then a hero would rise to lead the forces of light. But who was this hero? Where would they come from? And would they be ready when the time came?

The Legends of the Fallen

AS THE KINGDOM OF VALDORIA began to prepare for the inevitable conflict, the people turned to the legends of old for guidance. The tales of the fallen heroes who had once defended the land against the forces of darkness were told and retold in every corner of the kingdom. These stories, passed down through the generations, were filled with bravery, sacrifice, and the undying hope that good would triumph over evil.

One such legend was that of Seraphis the Valiant, a warrior of unmatched skill who had fought in the Great War of Shadows. Seraphis had led the armies of Valdoria against the dark sorcerer Malakar, who sought to plunge the world into eternal night. The battle had been fierce, and many lives were lost, but in the end, Seraphis had emerged victorious. However, the victory had come at a great cost. Seraphis was mortally wounded in the final battle, and with his dying breath, he had sworn that his blood would one day give rise to a new hero who would defend the kingdom in its darkest hour.

The tale of Seraphis was just one of many that spoke of heroes who had sacrificed everything for the greater good. These legends were more than just stories; they were a source of inspiration for the people of Valdoria, a reminder that even in the face of overwhelming odds, there was always hope.

But the prophecy of blood spoke of a different kind of hero—a hero born from the fallen, from the ashes of despair. This hero would not be like the warriors of legend, who had been born into greatness and trained from a young age to defend the kingdom. No, this hero would come from the most unlikely of places, and their journey would be fraught with hardship and loss.

As the people of Valdoria pondered the meaning of the prophecy, they could not help but wonder who this hero would be. Would they be a child born of noble blood, destined to carry on the legacy of their ancestors? Or would they be a commoner, rising from the depths of obscurity to fulfill their destiny? The answers were unclear, but one thing was certain—the time of the prophecy was drawing near, and the hero would soon be revealed.

The Mark of the Fallen

IN THE QUIET VILLAGE of Aeloria, far from the bustling streets of Eldoria, there lived a humble blacksmith named Kael. He was a man of few words, known for his skill with a hammer and his unwavering dedication to his craft. Kael had lived in Aeloria all his life, and though he was respected by his fellow villagers, he was not a man of great renown. He preferred the solitude of his forge, where he could work in peace and quiet, far from the troubles of the world.

But Kael carried a secret—a secret that even he did not fully understand. On the night of his birth, a strange mark had appeared on his chest, just above his heart. It was a mark that resembled the ancient symbols engraved on the altar in the Temple of Whispers, and it had been the cause of much fear and speculation among the villagers. Some believed it to be a curse, while others thought it to be a sign of great power. But Kael's parents, who were simple folk with no knowledge of prophecies or ancient magic, had chosen to keep the mark hidden, fearing that it would bring unwanted attention to their son.

As Kael grew older, he became aware of the mark's presence, but he did not understand its significance. He had never sought out the temple priests for answers, content to live his life as a blacksmith, far removed from the affairs of the kingdom. But as the signs of the prophecy began to manifest in the world around him, Kael could not shake the feeling that his life was about to change.

ONE EVENING, AS KAEL was closing up his forge for the night, he noticed a group of travelers approaching the village. They were dressed in tattered robes, their faces hidden by hoods, and they carried with them an air of mystery and danger. Kael watched as they made their way through the village, stopping at the inn to rest for the night. There was something about these travelers that unsettled him, but he could not quite put his finger on what it was.

The next morning, as Kael was preparing to open his forge, one of the travelers approached him. The man was tall and gaunt, with piercing blue eyes that seemed to see right through Kael. He introduced himself as Jareth, a wanderer and seeker of knowledge, and he asked Kael if he would repair his sword, which had been damaged in a recent battle.

Kael agreed, and as he examined the sword, he noticed that it was unlike any he had ever seen. The blade was made of a strange, black metal that seemed to absorb the light, and the hilt was adorned with symbols that matched the mark on Kael's chest. A sense of unease washed over him as he realized that this sword was connected to the prophecy in some way.

"Where did you get this sword?" Kael asked, his voice tense.

Jareth smiled, a knowing look in his eyes. "It was given to me by a great warrior," he replied. "A warrior who believed that one day, it would be wielded by a hero destined to save the kingdom."

Kael's heart raced as he listened to Jareth's words. Could it be that the prophecy was true, and that he was the hero spoken of in the ancient texts? The thought seemed impossible—he was just a simple blacksmith, with no training in the ways of war or magic. But the mark on his chest, and the sword that now lay before him, told a different story.

"I do not seek to be a hero," Kael said, his voice barely above a whisper. "I am just a man, with no desire for glory or power."

Jareth's expression softened, and he placed a hand on Kael's shoulder. "Sometimes, the greatest heroes are those who do not seek the mantle of heroism," he said. "The prophecy speaks of a hero born from the fallen—someone who has known loss and despair, but who rises above it to bring light to the darkness. The mark you bear is not a curse, but a sign that you are destined for something greater."

Kael looked down at the sword, his mind racing with thoughts of the prophecy and the role he was meant to play. He had never considered himself to be anything more than a blacksmith, but now, with the weight of the prophecy upon him, he could no longer deny that his life was about to change in ways he could never have imagined.

The Gathering Darkness

AS KAEL GRAPPLED WITH the revelations brought forth by Jareth, the forces of darkness continued to gather strength. In the far reaches of the kingdom, where the light of the sun barely touched the earth, a new threat was emerging. The dark sorcerer Malakar, thought to have been defeated centuries ago by Seraphis the Valiant, had returned, his power stronger than ever before.

Malakar had spent the centuries since his defeat in the shadows, gathering followers and honing his dark magic. He had sworn vengeance against Valdoria and its people, and he would stop at nothing to see the kingdom brought to its knees. His return marked the beginning of the prophecy's fulfillment, and he knew that the time of the blood moon was drawing near.

From his fortress in the Shadowlands, Malakar sent out his minions to sow fear and chaos across the kingdom. The earth trembled beneath their feet, and the skies darkened as they passed. Rivers that had once run clear now flowed red with blood, and the cries of the dying echoed through the land. These were the signs foretold in the prophecy, the harbingers of the coming battle.

But Malakar was not content to simply wait for the blood moon to rise. He knew that the prophecy spoke of a hero who would rise to challenge him, and he intended to find and eliminate this hero before they could fulfill their destiny. His spies scoured the kingdom, searching for any sign of the chosen one, while his dark magic reached out across the land, seeking to snuff out the light before it could shine.

In the quiet village of Aeloria, Kael was unaware of the forces that were converging upon him. He continued to work in his forge, the weight of the prophecy heavy on his mind. He had yet to tell anyone about the conversation he had had with Jareth, unsure of how to explain the strange feelings that had been stirred within him.

But as the days passed, Kael began to notice that things were not as they once were. The villagers, who had always been friendly and welcoming, now seemed distant and fearful. The once-clear skies were now shrouded in dark clouds, and the air was thick with tension. Kael could feel the darkness closing in, and he knew that it was only a matter of time before the battle foretold in the prophecy would begin.

One evening, as Kael was locking up his forge, he was approached by a group of villagers. Their faces were pale, their eyes wide with fear, and they spoke in hushed tones as they explained that strange things had been happening in the village. Livestock had gone missing, strange shadows had been seen moving through the fields at night, and the children had begun to have nightmares of a great darkness that was coming to devour them all.

Kael listened to their concerns, his heart heavy with the knowledge that these were the signs of the prophecy coming to pass. He had tried to ignore the growing sense of dread that had been building within him, but now it was impossible to deny that something was terribly wrong.

"We must do something," one of the villagers pleaded. "We cannot simply wait for this darkness to consume us. We must find a way to protect ourselves."

Kael nodded, his mind racing as he tried to think of a solution. He was just a blacksmith, with no knowledge of how to fight the forces of darkness. But he knew that he could no longer stand idly by while the prophecy unfolded around him.

"I will go to the temple," Kael said, his voice steady. "I will seek the counsel of the priests and see if they can help us understand what is happening."

The villagers nodded in agreement, their fear replaced by a flicker of hope. They trusted Kael, and they knew that if anyone could find a way to protect the village, it was him.

As Kael prepared to leave for the temple, he felt a strange sense of calm settle over him. He knew that the journey ahead would be dangerous, and that the answers he sought might not be what he hoped for. But he also knew that he could no longer ignore the prophecy, or the role that he was destined to play in the coming battle.

The Journey to the Temple

THE ROAD TO THE TEMPLE of Whispers was long and treacherous, winding through dense forests and over steep mountains. Kael traveled alone, his only companions the thoughts that weighed heavily on his mind. The mark on his chest, once a source of fear and confusion, now seemed to pulse with a life of its own, as if it was guiding him toward his destiny.

As Kael journeyed through the wilderness, he encountered signs of the darkness that was spreading across the land. The trees, once vibrant and green, were now withered and dying, their branches twisted into grotesque shapes. The rivers, once clear and pure, were now choked with blood and debris. And the air, once filled with the songs of birds and the rustling of leaves, was now silent, as if the world itself was holding its breath in anticipation of the coming battle.

Despite the ominous signs, Kael pressed on, determined to reach the temple and find the answers he sought. He knew that the priests who guarded the temple possessed ancient knowledge and wisdom, and that they might be able to shed light on the prophecy and his role in it.

After several days of travel, Kael finally arrived at the Temple of Whispers. The sight of the ancient structure, carved into the side of the mountain, filled him with a sense of awe and reverence. The temple was as old as the kingdom itself, its stone walls bearing the marks of countless generations of priests who had come before him.

Kael approached the temple's entrance, his footsteps echoing on the cold stone. As he stepped inside, he was greeted by the flickering light of torches and the faint scent of incense. The interior of the temple was dimly lit, the shadows dancing on the walls as the flames flickered in the breeze.

At the center of the temple, Kael saw the stone altar where the prophecy had first been uttered. The ancient symbols engraved on its surface seemed to glow with an otherworldly light, as if they were calling out to him. Kael felt a strange compulsion to approach the altar, and as he did, he could feel the mark on his chest burning with a fierce intensity.

As he reached the altar, Kael was approached by the High Priestess, the same woman who had spoken the prophecy all those years ago. She was old and frail, her eyes clouded by time, but there was a wisdom in her gaze that made Kael feel as if she could see into his very soul.

"You have come, as I knew you would," the High Priestess said, her voice barely above a whisper. "The time of the prophecy is upon us, and you are the one who will decide the fate of the kingdom."

Kael bowed his head, humbled by the weight of her words.

"I do not know if I am the hero spoken of in the prophecy," he said, his voice filled with doubt. "I am just a simple blacksmith, with no knowledge of how to fight the forces of darkness."

The High Priestess smiled, a look of understanding in her eyes. "The prophecy does not speak of a hero born of greatness," she said. "It speaks of a hero born from the fallen, from the ashes of despair. You have known loss and hardship, but you have also known strength and resilience. The mark you bear is a sign that you are destined for something greater."

Kael looked down at the mark on his chest, the ancient symbol glowing with a soft, golden light. He had always seen it as a curse, a mark of shame that he had tried to hide from the world. But now, as he stood before the High Priestess, he realized that it was not a curse, but a gift—a gift that would allow him to fulfill his destiny.

"What must I do?" Kael asked, his voice filled with determination.

The High Priestess reached out and placed her hand on Kael's chest, over the mark. "You must embrace your destiny," she said. "The time of the blood moon is drawing near, and the forces of darkness are gathering. You must find the Sword of Legends, the only weapon that can alter the course of fate, and you must lead the forces of light against the darkness."

Kael nodded, his resolve strengthening with each passing moment. He knew that the journey ahead would be difficult, and that the path he was about to walk would be fraught with danger. But he also knew that he could no longer turn back.

"I will do whatever it takes to protect the kingdom," Kael said, his voice filled with conviction.

The High Priestess smiled, a look of pride in her eyes. "Then go, Kael of Aeloria," she said. "Go and fulfill your destiny. The fate of the kingdom rests in your hands."

The Rise of the Hero

AS KAEL LEFT THE TEMPLE, his heart was filled with a sense of purpose that he had never known before. He was no longer just a simple blacksmith, content to live his life in obscurity. He was the hero spoken of in the prophecy, destined to lead the forces of light against the darkness.

But Kael knew that he could not do it alone. He would need allies, warriors who would stand by his side in the coming battle. And he would need the Sword of Legends, the only weapon capable of defeating the dark sorcerer Malakar.

Kael set out on his journey, determined to find the sword and gather the forces he would need to protect the kingdom. As he traveled through the kingdom of Valdoria, he encountered many who had heard of the prophecy and were eager to join his cause. Warriors, mages, and scholars all pledged their loyalty to Kael, ready to fight for the future of the kingdom.

Word of Kael's quest soon spread throughout the land, and it was not long before the people of Valdoria began to see him as the hero they had been waiting for. The legends of old spoke of great warriors who had defended the kingdom in its darkest hour, but Kael was different. He was not born into greatness, but had risen from the ashes of despair to embrace his destiny.

As Kael's army grew, so too did the forces of darkness. Malakar's minions continued to spread fear and chaos across the land, and the blood moon drew ever closer. The stage was set for the battle foretold in the prophecy—a battle that would decide the fate of the kingdom.

But even as Kael prepared for the coming conflict, he could not shake the feeling that there was something he was missing—some crucial piece of the puzzle that had yet to reveal itself. The prophecy had spoken of a hero who would rise from the fallen, but it had also warned of the dangers that lay ahead. The line between light and darkness was thin, and Kael knew that one wrong move could plunge the world into eternal night.

As the blood moon began to rise in the sky, casting its ominous red glow over the land, Kael knew that the time had come. The prophecy was about to be fulfilled, and the fate of the kingdom rested on his shoulders.

With the Sword of Legends in hand and his army at his back, Kael marched toward the battlefield, ready to face the darkness and fulfill his destiny.

The battle of blood and fire was about to begin.

End of Chapter 1

Chapter 2: The Birth of the Chosen

The Village of Shadows

Hidden deep within the veil of the Orinthian Mountains, where the towering peaks seemed to touch the sky and the dense forests whispered secrets of old, there lay a village so remote that its existence was known to only a few. This village, called Shadows' Rest by its inhabitants, had been deliberately kept out of the kingdom's knowledge for generations. It was a place where time moved slowly, and where the outside world's troubles rarely penetrated the thick canopy of trees that shielded it from view.

The people of Shadows' Rest were an enigmatic folk, living simple lives in harmony with the land. They were farmers, hunters, and craftsmen, content with the quiet life their isolation afforded them. But beneath their simple exterior lay an ancient duty—one that bound them to the prophecy of blood that was whispered among the learned and feared by the wise. For Shadows' Rest was not just any village; it was a place of refuge, a sanctuary for those whose lives were touched by destiny.

The village had been founded centuries ago by a group of people who sought to protect a lineage foretold by the seers. They knew that one day, from their midst, a child would be born who would carry the burden of the world's fate upon their shoulders. This knowledge was passed down through the generations, a sacred trust that bound the villagers together in their mission to shield the chosen one from the eyes of those who would seek to use or destroy them.

And so, when the signs of the prophecy began to manifest in the world beyond—the trembling earth, the darkened skies, and the rivers running red—the villagers of Shadows' Rest knew that the time was near. They had prepared for this moment for centuries, and now, they could only wait for the child of destiny to be born.

The Mysterious Night

IT WAS A NIGHT UNLIKE any other, when the sky itself seemed to hold its breath. The moon, usually a gentle beacon of silver light, had taken on a crimson hue, bathing the village in an eerie glow. The air was thick with anticipation, and even the animals in the surrounding forest were unnervingly silent, as if they too sensed that something monumental was about to occur.

In a small, humble cottage at the edge of the village, a woman named Elara lay in her bed, her breath coming in quick, shallow gasps. She was a strong woman, a healer by trade, known for her calm demeanor and steady hands. But on this night, she was neither calm nor steady, for she was in the throes of childbirth.

Elara's husband, a kind and gentle man named Caelan, paced anxiously at her bedside. His face was pale with worry, and his hands trembled as he held his wife's hand. They had longed for this child for many years, and now, as the moment approached, fear gnawed at his heart. He knew, as did the rest of the villagers, that this was no ordinary birth.

The midwife, a stoic woman named Eirlys, worked with practiced efficiency, her hands moving with the surety of someone who had delivered countless children into the world. But even she could not shake the feeling that something was different about this birth. The air in the room was charged with a strange energy, and the crimson light of the moon seemed to pulse in time with Elara's labored breathing.

"Steady, Elara," Eirlys murmured, her voice soothing yet firm. "You're doing well. The child is almost here."

Elara nodded weakly, her grip tightening on Caelan's hand. She had known from the moment she first felt the child stir within her womb that this was no ordinary pregnancy. There had been signs—dreams of a world engulfed in darkness, of a great battle waged on fields stained with blood, and of a child standing at the center of it all, bearing the weight of an unimaginable destiny.

She had kept these dreams to herself, sharing them only with Caelan, who had tried to comfort her with assurances that they were merely the imaginings of an expectant mother. But as the months passed and the signs in the world around them grew more pronounced, Elara knew that her dreams were not just dreams. They were visions of the future, glimpses of a fate that had already been set in motion long before she or her child had come into existence.

As another wave of pain wracked her body, Elara cried out, her voice echoing through the small cottage. Eirlys moved swiftly, guiding the child into the world with the skill of a master. And then, with a final push, the child was born.

For a moment, there was silence. The world seemed to hold its breath as Eirlys lifted the newborn into her arms, her eyes widening as she gazed upon the child. The infant's skin was as pale as the winter snow, and a thick shock of raven-black hair covered their head. But it was the child's eyes that truly marked them as different—eyes the color of molten gold, glowing with an inner light that seemed to pierce the very soul.

Eirlys, usually unshakable in her duties, felt a tremor of awe and fear as she held the child. She had seen many babies born in her lifetime, but none like this. The child radiated a power that was both mesmerizing and terrifying, a power that she knew could only mean one thing.

"The prophecy…" Eirlys whispered, her voice trembling as she looked at Elara and Caelan. "This child…they are the one."

Caelan's breath caught in his throat as he looked at his newborn child, cradled in the midwife's arms. He had heard the tales, the whispered legends of a child who would be born under the blood moon, marked by the signs of the prophecy. But he had never truly believed that such a thing could happen to them, to their family.

Elara, exhausted but still aware of the significance of the moment, reached out for her child. Eirlys hesitated for only a moment before placing the baby in her arms, her hands lingering as if reluctant to let go of the child who carried the fate of the world.

As Elara gazed down at her newborn, tears filled her eyes. The child looked up at her with those glowing golden eyes, and in that moment, Elara felt a connection so deep, so profound, that it took her breath away. This child was hers, but they were also so much more. They were the one spoken of in the ancient texts, the one who would rise from the fallen to lead the forces of light against the darkness.

"Elara," Caelan whispered, his voice filled with awe and fear. "What are we to do?"

Elara looked at her husband, her heart heavy with the knowledge of what lay ahead. They had both known that their lives would change with the birth of their child, but they had not been prepared for this. Their child was not just theirs; they belonged to the world, to the prophecy that had been set in motion long before they were born.

"We must protect them," Elara said, her voice steady despite the fear that gripped her heart. "We must keep their identity hidden from the world, until the time is right. The prophecy must be fulfilled, but we cannot allow our child to be taken before they are ready."

Caelan nodded, his resolve strengthening as he looked at his wife and child. He had always known that Elara was strong, but in that moment, he realized just how strong she truly was. Together, they would do whatever it took to protect their child, to ensure that the prophecy would be fulfilled when the time came.

The Mark of Destiny

AS THE DAYS TURNED into weeks, and the weeks into months, the villagers of Shadows' Rest watched the child with a mixture of awe and fear. The baby, whom Elara and Caelan had named Eryndor, grew quickly, their golden eyes always observing, always seeming to see more than a child their age should.

The villagers had been sworn to secrecy, bound by the ancient oath that had been passed down through the generations. They knew that Eryndor was special, that they were the one spoken of in the prophecy, but they also knew that revealing this knowledge to the outside world would put the child in grave danger.

And so, they did their best to raise Eryndor as any other child, though it was clear from the beginning that they were anything but ordinary. Eryndor possessed an intelligence far beyond their years, and a curiosity that could not be sated. They would often disappear into the forests surrounding the village, only to return with stories of strange creatures and hidden glades that no one else had ever seen.

But it was not just Eryndor's intellect that set them apart. As they grew, it became clear that they possessed abilities that no other child in the village had. They could heal wounds with a touch, speak to animals as if they understood their language, and even manipulate the elements—summoning fire from the tips of their fingers or calling down rain from a clear sky.

These abilities, while remarkable, also served as a constant reminder of the prophecy that hung over their heads like a dark cloud. The villagers feared for Eryndor's safety, knowing that if word of their powers reached the outside world, it would only be a matter of time before those who sought to control or destroy them would come.

Elara and Caelan did their best to protect Eryndor, teaching them to hide their abilities and to never reveal the mark they bore on their chest—a mark that had appeared on the night of their birth, identical to the one described in the ancient texts. It was a mark that signified their role in the prophecy, a mark that could not be erased or hidden for long.

But even as they tried to shield their child from the dangers that lay beyond the village, Elara and Caelan knew that they could not keep Eryndor hidden forever. The world was changing, the signs of the prophecy growing more pronounced with each passing day. The darkness was gathering, and soon, Eryndor would have to leave the safety of Shadows' Rest to fulfill their destiny.

The Threat from Beyond

IT WAS DURING ERYNDOR'S twelfth year that the first true threat to their safety emerged. Word had reached the village that a group of strangers had been seen in the surrounding forests, asking questions about a child born under the blood moon. These strangers were not ordinary travelers; they were agents of the dark sorcerer Malakar, sent to find the chosen one and bring them to him, dead or alive.

The villagers were terrified. They had lived in peace for generations, far from the prying eyes of the outside world. But now, that peace was shattered, and the shadow of the prophecy loomed larger than ever before.

Elara and Caelan knew that they had to act quickly. They could not allow Eryndor to fall into Malakar's hands, not when the fate of the kingdom rested on their shoulders. And so, they made a decision that would change their lives forever.

"We must leave," Elara said, her voice trembling with fear and determination. "We must take Eryndor and flee before they find us."

Caelan nodded, his heart heavy with the weight of what they were about to do. Leaving Shadows' Rest meant leaving behind the only life they had ever known, the only place where they had felt safe. But they had no choice. The prophecy was in motion, and they had to protect their child at all costs.

That night, under the cover of darkness, Elara and Caelan gathered what few belongings they could carry and set out with Eryndor into the wilderness. They traveled by the light of the blood moon, its crimson glow guiding their way as they made their way through the dense forests and treacherous mountain passes.

Eryndor, though young, understood the gravity of the situation. They had always known that they were different, that they were destined for something greater than the simple life they had lived in Shadows' Rest. But now, as they left behind the only home they had ever known, they realized just how much their life was about to change.

As they traveled, Elara and Caelan told Eryndor the truth about the prophecy and their role in it. They explained that they were the chosen one, destined to lead the forces of light against the darkness. They spoke of the great battle that was to come, of the sword that Eryndor would have to find, and of the enemies who would stop at nothing to see them destroyed.

Eryndor listened in silence, their golden eyes wide with a mixture of fear and determination. They had always felt that there was something different about them, something that set them apart from the other children in the village. But to hear it spoken aloud, to know that they were the one who would decide the fate of the world, was almost too much to comprehend.

"Do not be afraid," Elara said, sensing her child's fear. "You are strong, stronger than you know. We will protect you, and when the time comes, you will fulfill your destiny."

Eryndor nodded, though the fear in their heart was still present. They did not want to be a hero; they did not want to carry the burden of the world's fate on their shoulders. But they also knew that they had no choice. The prophecy had chosen them, and they could not turn away from their destiny.

The Guardians of the Light

AFTER MANY DAYS OF travel, Elara, Caelan, and Eryndor arrived at the hidden sanctuary of the Guardians of the Light. The Guardians were a secretive order, dedicated to the protection of the chosen one and the fulfillment of the prophecy. They had been waiting for Eryndor's arrival for many years, and they welcomed the family with open arms.

The sanctuary was a place of peace and tranquility, hidden deep within the heart of the mountains. It was a place where the forces of darkness could not reach, protected by ancient wards and powerful magic. Here, Eryndor would be safe, and here, they would begin their training for the battle that lay ahead.

The leader of the Guardians, a wise and powerful sorceress named Seraphina, took Eryndor under her wing. She had known of the prophecy since she was a young girl, and she had dedicated her life to preparing for the chosen one's arrival. Now, as she looked at the young child before her, she knew that the time had come.

"You have a great destiny, Eryndor," Seraphina said, her voice gentle but firm. "But with that destiny comes great responsibility. The world will look to you in its darkest hour, and you must be ready to lead."

Eryndor looked up at Seraphina, their golden eyes filled with determination. "I will do whatever it takes," they said, their voice steady. "I will not let the darkness win."

Seraphina smiled, a sense of pride swelling in her heart. "Good," she said. "But remember, you are not alone. The Guardians are here to guide you, to teach you. Together, we will prepare for the battle that is to come."

And so, Eryndor began their training. Under Seraphina's guidance, they learned to harness their abilities, to control the power that flowed through their veins. They trained in the arts of magic and combat, learning to wield both the sword and the spell with equal proficiency.

But more than that, they learned the importance of wisdom, of knowing when to fight and when to seek peace. Seraphina taught them that true strength did not come from power alone, but from the heart, from the courage to do what was right even in the face of overwhelming odds.

As the months turned into years, Eryndor grew into a formidable warrior, a leader who inspired loyalty and courage in those around them. They were no longer the frightened child who had fled from Shadows' Rest; they were the chosen one, destined to lead the forces of light against the darkness.

But even as they prepared for the battle to come, Eryndor knew that their journey was far from over. The prophecy was still unfolding, and the world was changing. The darkness was growing stronger, and the time of the blood moon was drawing near.

And as the day of the great battle approached, Eryndor could not shake the feeling that their destiny was not just to fight, but to unite—to bring together the forces of light in a way that had never been done before. They knew that the battle would be difficult, that they would face challenges and sacrifices unlike any they had ever known. But they also knew that they were not alone.

With the Guardians by their side, and the knowledge of their destiny guiding their path, Eryndor was ready to face whatever the future held.

The child of prophecy had been born, and the world would never be the same.

End of Chapter 2

Chapter 3: The Gathering Storm

The Prophecy Echoes Beyond Valdoria

The prophecy of blood had always been a closely guarded secret, whispered in the ancient halls of Valdoria and recorded in the sacred texts of the Temple of Whispers. But prophecies have a way of spreading beyond their point of origin, carried on the winds of rumor, and fed by the fears of those who sense that the world is about to change. The prophecy of blood was no different. As the signs foretold in the prophecy began to manifest—the trembling earth, the blood-red rivers, and the darkened skies—the neighboring kingdoms could not help but take notice.

These kingdoms, each with their own history and traditions, had long been aware of the power and mystique surrounding Valdoria. They had heard the legends of the great battles fought by Valdorian heroes, of the ancient magics that flowed through its lands, and of the mysterious prophecies that had guided its people through the ages. But now, with the prophecy of blood coming to the forefront, these kingdoms found themselves drawn into a storm of uncertainty and fear.

In the kingdom of Eloria to the west, the royal court buzzed with speculation about the meaning of the signs. The Elorians were a people of tradition and order, ruled by a council of elders who placed great value on the interpretation of omens and prophecies. The signs that had begun to appear in their own lands—the darkened skies, the restless earth, and the strange behavior of the animals—could not be ignored. The council gathered in the Grand Hall of Elders, their faces etched with concern as they debated the implications of the prophecy.

"These signs are a warning," declared Elder Mora, a venerable figure with a long white beard and sharp, piercing eyes. "The prophecy of blood speaks of a great battle that will decide the fate of kingdoms. We cannot afford to be unprepared."

"But what does the prophecy truly mean?" asked Elder Lyra, a younger woman with a keen intellect and a skeptical nature. "Is it a warning, a call to arms, or perhaps a test of our resolve? We must be cautious in our interpretation."

Elder Mora stroked his beard thoughtfully. "The prophecy is clear: a hero will rise from the fallen, and the forces of darkness will gather to challenge the light. We must assume that this battle will affect all the kingdoms, not just Valdoria."

"The question is," interjected Elder Alaric, a stern man with a military bearing, "how do we respond? Do we prepare for war, or do we seek alliances to protect ourselves from whatever may come?"

The council fell silent, each member lost in their thoughts. The Elorians had always prided themselves on their wisdom and caution, but now, faced with the uncertainty of the prophecy, they found themselves divided. Some, like Elder Mora, believed that they must prepare for war, while others, like Elder Lyra, urged a more measured approach.

"Perhaps," suggested Elder Lyra, "we should seek counsel from Valdoria. The prophecy originated there, and they may have more insight into its meaning. If we are to face this challenge, we must do so with as much knowledge as possible."

Elder Mora nodded slowly. "You may be right, Lyra. We will send an envoy to Valdoria to learn what we can. In the meantime, we must begin preparations. If war is coming, we cannot be caught off guard."

And so, the kingdom of Eloria began to prepare for the gathering storm, sending emissaries to Valdoria while quietly readying their defenses. The council's decision to seek knowledge rather than rush into conflict was a reflection of their cautious nature, but even they could sense that the time for action was drawing near.

The Flames of War in Drakoria

TO THE EAST OF VALDORIA lay the kingdom of Drakoria, a land of fierce warriors and proud traditions. The Drakorians were known for their strength in battle, their loyalty to their king, and their deep connection to the dragons that roamed their lands. The prophecy of blood, with its promise of a great battle, resonated deeply with the Drakorian people, who saw it as a call to arms, a chance to prove their might on the field of battle.

King Raegon, the ruler of Drakoria, was a man of action. He had ascended to the throne through strength and cunning, and he was not one to shy away from conflict. When the signs of the prophecy began to appear in Drakoria—the tremors that shook the earth, the crimson skies that bled over the horizon, and the dragons that grew restless in their mountain lairs—Raegon saw them not as warnings, but as omens of glory.

"The time has come," Raegon declared to his assembled war council, his voice echoing through the grand chamber of his fortress. "The prophecy speaks of a great battle, and we Drakorians are born for battle! We will not wait for the darkness to come to us. We will take the fight to them, and we will prove our strength to all the kingdoms!"

The warlords who sat at the king's table nodded in agreement, their eyes gleaming with the anticipation of battle. Among them was General Kaelen, a seasoned warrior who had fought in countless campaigns and had earned his place as the king's most trusted commander.

"Your Majesty," Kaelen said, his voice steady and confident, "our forces are ready. The legions are strong, the dragons are restless, and the people are eager for battle. We have long waited for an opportunity to expand our borders, and this prophecy may be the key to achieving that goal."

Raegon smiled, a fierce light in his eyes. "Then we shall not waste any time. Send word to our allies. We will forge new alliances, gather our strength, and prepare to march on Valdoria. The prophecy may speak of a hero who will rise from the fallen, but it is the strong who will decide the fate of this world!"

As the war council began to make plans for the coming campaign, Raegon felt a surge of excitement. He had always believed that destiny favored the bold, and now, with the prophecy as his guide, he was determined to carve out a new future for Drakoria—one in which his kingdom would reign supreme.

But Raegon was not a fool. He knew that the other kingdoms would not sit idly by while Drakoria marched to war. He would need to secure his borders, neutralize potential threats, and ensure that his allies were firmly in his grasp.

The flames of war had been ignited, and Raegon intended to fan them into an inferno that would consume all who stood in his way.

The Awakening of the Old Gods in Thaloria

TO THE NORTH OF VALDORIA lay the kingdom of Thaloria, a land steeped in ancient traditions and shrouded in mystery. The Thalorians were a deeply spiritual people, their lives guided by the teachings of the Old Gods—ancient deities who had once walked the earth and whose power still lingered in the sacred groves and hidden temples of the land.

The prophecy of blood, with its promise of a great battle between light and darkness, resonated with the Thalorian belief in the eternal struggle between order and chaos. But unlike the other kingdoms, the Thalorians did not see the prophecy as a mere omen of war. They saw it as a sign that the Old Gods were awakening, that the time had come for the ancient powers to rise once more and reclaim their dominion over the world.

High Priestess Isolde, the spiritual leader of Thaloria, stood in the heart of the Sacred Grove, her hands raised to the heavens as she communed with the Old Gods. The grove was a place of immense power, where the veil between the mortal world and the realm of the gods was thin. The air was thick with the scent of incense and the soft glow of magical lights that danced among the trees.

As Isolde chanted the ancient hymns, her voice resonating with the power of the Old Gods, she felt a presence stirring within the grove. It was a presence she had not felt in centuries, a force so ancient and powerful that it sent a shiver down her spine.

"Great Ones," Isolde whispered, her voice trembling with reverence. "The time has come, has it not? The prophecy speaks of a great battle, of a hero who will rise from the fallen. What would you have us do?"

The air in the grove grew still, and for a moment, Isolde feared that the gods would not answer. But then, a voice echoed through the trees, a voice that was both ancient and eternal.

"The time of reckoning is at hand, daughter of Thaloria," the voice intoned. "The world teeters on the brink of chaos, and the forces of light and darkness prepare for war. But know this: the true battle is not between mortal kingdoms, but between the powers that have long slumbered. The Old Gods must awaken, and the world must be reminded of their might."

Isolde bowed her head, her heart pounding in her chest. The Old Gods had spoken, and their will was clear. The prophecy was not just a call to arms; it was a call to awaken the ancient powers that had once ruled the world.

"We will do as you command, Great Ones," Isolde vowed. "We will awaken the Old Gods, and we will prepare for the battle that is to come. The world will know the power of Thaloria, and the Old Gods will rise once more."

With her vow made, Isolde left the Sacred Grove and returned to the Temple of the Old Gods, where the priests and priestesses awaited her return. She could see the tension in their faces, the uncertainty that lingered in their hearts. They had all felt the stirring of the Old Gods, and they knew that something monumental was about to occur.

"The Old Gods have spoken," Isolde announced, her voice filled with the authority of the divine. "The prophecy is not just a warning of war—it is a call to awaken the ancient powers that have long slumbered. We must prepare the rites, summon the spirits, and awaken the Old Gods from their sleep. The world must know that the power of Thaloria still reigns."

The priests and priestesses bowed their heads in agreement, their fear replaced by a sense of purpose. The Old Gods were awakening, and with their power, Thaloria would rise to meet the coming storm.

As the preparations began, Isolde could not help but feel a sense of awe and dread. The Old Gods were ancient and powerful, but they were also unpredictable. Their awakening would bring great power, but it would also bring great danger. The world was on the brink of a new era, one that would be shaped by forces beyond mortal comprehension.

The Machinations of the Shadow Council in Umbrosia

TO THE SOUTH OF VALDORIA lay the shadowy kingdom of Umbrosia, a land of darkness and intrigue where secrets were currency and power was wielded from the shadows. The Umbrosians were a people of cunning and guile, ruled by the enigmatic Shadow Council—a group of powerful individuals who manipulated the affairs of the kingdom from behind the scenes.

The prophecy of blood, with its promise of a great battle between light and darkness, was of particular interest to the Shadow Council. They had long known of the prophecy, having obtained ancient texts and relics through their vast network of spies and informants. But to the Umbrosians, the prophecy was not just a prediction of war—it was an opportunity.

The Shadow Council convened in a dimly lit chamber deep within the heart of the capital city of Umbra. The room was shrouded in darkness, with only the faint glow of magical orbs providing any illumination. The members of the council, each cloaked in shadow, sat in silence as their leader, known only as the Shadowmaster, spoke.

"The prophecy of blood has begun to unfold," the Shadowmaster said, his voice low and measured. "The kingdoms are preparing for war, and the forces of darkness are gathering. But where others see chaos, we see opportunity. The prophecy is a tool, one that we can use to our advantage."

The council members nodded in agreement, their faces hidden in the darkness. They were all masters of manipulation, skilled in the art of deception and intrigue. They had risen to power by exploiting the weaknesses of others, and they saw the prophecy as just another tool in their arsenal.

"The neighboring kingdoms are already preparing for conflict," the Shadowmaster continued. "Eloria seeks knowledge, Drakoria seeks conquest, and Thaloria seeks to awaken its ancient gods. Each of them has their own interpretation of the prophecy, and each of them is blinded by their own ambitions. We will use this to our advantage."

"But what of Valdoria?" asked one of the council members, her voice smooth and calculating. "They are the heart of the prophecy. Should we not be concerned about their chosen hero?"

The Shadowmaster smiled, a cold and calculating smile that sent a shiver through the chamber. "Valdoria is indeed at the center of the prophecy, but they are also vulnerable. The chosen hero is young, untested. We have eyes and ears within Valdoria, and we will ensure that the hero is neutralized before they can become a threat."

The council member nodded in satisfaction. The Shadow Council had long cultivated a network of spies and informants within Valdoria, and they were confident in their ability to manipulate events to their advantage.

"In the meantime," the Shadowmaster said, his voice taking on a more serious tone, "we must ensure that the other kingdoms remain divided. We will sow discord among them, pit them against each other, and weaken their resolve. The prophecy speaks of a great battle, but it does not say who will emerge victorious. We will ensure that Umbrosia is the one that stands triumphant when the dust settles."

The council members murmured their agreement, their minds already racing with plans and schemes. The Shadow Council thrived on chaos and conflict, and the prophecy of blood had provided them with the perfect opportunity to extend their influence and power.

As the council began to discuss their plans in more detail, the Shadowmaster leaned back in his chair, a sense of satisfaction washing over him. The prophecy was a powerful force, one that could shape the destiny of kingdoms. But in the hands of the Shadow Council, it was also a weapon—a weapon that could be used to bring the world under their control.

The Awakening of the Dark Forces

WHILE THE KINGDOMS of Valdoria, Eloria, Drakoria, Thaloria, and Umbrosia each prepared for the coming storm in their own way, there were other forces at work—forces that had long slumbered in the depths of the earth, waiting for the right moment to rise.

Deep beneath the surface of the world, in the forgotten caverns and ancient ruins that had been lost to time, the dark forces that had once threatened the world began to stir. These were the forces of the ancient sorcerer Malakar, the dark lord who had nearly plunged the world into eternal night centuries ago. Though Malakar had been defeated by the hero Seraphis, his power had not been entirely extinguished. It had merely been dormant, waiting for the time of the prophecy to awaken once more.

In the darkest corners of the world, where the light of the sun could not reach, Malakar's minions began to emerge. These were creatures of shadow and darkness, twisted by the dark magic that had once fueled Malakar's ambitions. They were the remnants of his army, the servants who had sworn to bring about the destruction of the world in the name of their master.

The first of these dark forces to awaken was the Shadow Legion, an army of spectral warriors who had once served as Malakar's elite guard. Bound to their master by dark magic, they had been entombed in the Black Vault, a forgotten prison deep beneath the earth. But now, as the prophecy began to unfold, the seals on the Black Vault weakened, and the Shadow Legion began to stir.

The Shadow Legion was led by a figure known only as the Dark Captain, a warrior of immense power and cruelty. He had been Malakar's most trusted commander, leading the sorcerer's forces into battle during the Great War of Shadows. Though his body had long since turned to dust, his spirit remained bound to the dark magic that had sustained him in life. Now, with the prophecy of blood drawing near, the Dark Captain and his legion were ready to rise once more.

But the Shadow Legion was not the only force to awaken. In the depths of the Abyssal Caves, the Wraith King stirred from his ancient slumber. The Wraith King had once been a mighty sorcerer, a rival to Malakar who had sought to claim the world for himself. But Malakar had defeated him, imprisoning him in the Abyssal Caves and binding his soul to the darkness. Now, with the prophecy drawing near, the Wraith King sensed that his time had come. He would rise once more, and this time, he would not be denied.

In the northern wastes, where the cold winds howled and the sun never rose, the Frost Giants began to awaken from their long sleep. These ancient beings had once ruled the north, their power unmatched by any mortal force. But they had been defeated by the combined might of the kingdoms, and they had retreated into the frozen wastes, where they had slumbered for centuries. But now, the prophecy had reached even their frozen hearts, and they knew that the time had come to reclaim their lost dominion.

As these dark forces began to stir, the world trembled. The kingdoms, each preparing for the prophecy in their own way, were unaware of the true danger that was awakening beneath their feet. The prophecy of blood spoke of a great battle, but it did not reveal the true scope of the conflict that was about to unfold.

For this was not just a battle between kingdoms—it was a battle between the forces of light and darkness, between the ancient powers that had shaped the world and the heroes who would rise to defend it.

The First Clashes

AS THE KINGDOMS PREPARED for war, the first skirmishes began to break out along their borders. In the forests that lay between Valdoria and Eloria, scouts from both kingdoms clashed in brief but fierce encounters. Neither side sought full-scale conflict, but tensions were high, and misunderstandings could easily spiral into violence.

In the skies above Drakoria, the dragons grew restless, their roars echoing across the mountains as they sensed the coming conflict. The Drakorian legions began to mobilize, their armor gleaming in the sunlight as they prepared to march on Valdoria. Raegon's war machine was in motion, and the king was eager to test his might against the forces of darkness.

In the sacred groves of Thaloria, the rites to awaken the Old Gods were well underway. High Priestess Isolde led her followers in ancient rituals, calling upon the spirits of the land to rise and join the battle. The air crackled with magic, and the very earth seemed to pulse with the power of the Old Gods.

In the shadowy streets of Umbrosia, the agents of the Shadow Council moved unseen, spreading rumors and misinformation to sow discord among the other kingdoms. They whispered of betrayals and secret alliances, fanning the flames of suspicion and mistrust. The Shadowmaster watched from the darkness, pleased with the chaos that was beginning to unfold.

But it was in the depths of the earth, in the forgotten places where the dark forces had slumbered, that the true danger lay. The Shadow Legion, the Wraith King, and the Frost Giants were awakening, their power growing with each passing day. They would soon emerge from the darkness, and when they did, the world would tremble.

The Calm Before the Storm

AS THE KINGDOMS PREPARED for war, a sense of unease settled over the land. The signs of the prophecy were everywhere—the trembling earth, the blood-red rivers, the darkened skies. The people whispered of the coming battle, of the hero who would rise to lead them, and of the darkness that threatened to consume them all.

In Valdoria, Eryndor continued their training with the Guardians of the Light, their resolve growing stronger with each passing day. They knew that the time was near, that the prophecy was unfolding, and that they would soon be called upon to fulfill their destiny.

But even as Eryndor prepared for the battle to come, they could not shake the feeling that something was amiss. The world was changing, and the forces at play were far greater than anything they had imagined. The prophecy spoke of a great battle, but it did not reveal the true nature of the conflict that was about to unfold.

For this was not just a battle between kingdoms—it was a battle between light and darkness, between the ancient powers that had shaped the world and the heroes who would rise to defend it.

And as the storm clouds gathered on the horizon, the world held its breath, waiting for the first clash of steel, the first cry of battle, and the first drop of blood that would herald the beginning of the end.

The Gathering Storm had begun.

End of Chapter 3

Chapter 4: The Sword of Legends

The Call to Quest

Eryndor stood atop the ancient battlements of the Guardian's stronghold, gazing out over the vast landscape that stretched beyond the mountains. The sun was setting, casting a golden hue across the sky, and the distant peaks were shrouded in the twilight's gentle embrace. But despite the beauty of the scene before them, Eryndor's mind was troubled, consumed by thoughts of the prophecy and the role they were destined to play in the coming battle.

The prophecy had been a constant presence in Eryndor's life, a shadow that loomed over every decision, every action. But now, as the signs of the prophecy continued to manifest and the world edged closer to war, the weight of that destiny felt heavier than ever. Eryndor knew that they could not delay any longer. The time had come to seek out the one weapon that could tip the scales in the battle against darkness—the Sword of Legends.

This sword, spoken of in the oldest texts and whispered about in tales passed down through generations, was said to be forged by the first heroes, blessed with the power to vanquish any foe and to turn the tide of even the most dire of conflicts. Its location, however, had been lost to time, hidden away in a place where only the truly worthy could find it.

The Sword of Legends was more than just a weapon—it was a symbol of hope, of the light that could overcome even the deepest darkness. But to find it, Eryndor knew they would have to undertake a perilous journey, one that would test not only their strength but also their courage, wisdom, and resolve.

As Eryndor stood on the battlements, they felt a presence behind them. Turning, they saw Seraphina, the leader of the Guardians, approaching. Her expression was calm, but her eyes held a seriousness that Eryndor had come to recognize as a sign that something important was about to be said.

"You're troubled," Seraphina said, her voice soft but firm.

Eryndor nodded, unable to hide the anxiety that had been building within them. "The time is drawing near," they replied. "I know what I must do, but the path ahead is unclear. The Sword of Legends... how am I to find it when so many before me have failed?"

Seraphina placed a comforting hand on Eryndor's shoulder. "The path of the chosen one has never been an easy one, Eryndor. The legends speak of many who sought the sword, but only those with a pure heart, a sharp mind, and unyielding resolve could ever hope to find it. This quest will test you in ways you cannot yet imagine, but it is also an opportunity for you to grow, to discover the strength within yourself that will be necessary to fulfill your destiny."

Eryndor looked into Seraphina's eyes, finding solace in her wisdom and strength. "Where do I begin?" they asked, their voice filled with determination.

"The sword is said to be hidden in the Valley of Echoes, a place where time and space converge, and where the past and present intertwine," Seraphina explained. "The valley is located deep within the mountains, far beyond the borders of Valdoria. But be warned—reaching the valley is only the first step. The sword is protected by ancient guardians, and you will face trials that will challenge not just your body, but your spirit and mind as well."

Eryndor nodded, understanding the gravity of the task before them. "I will do whatever it takes to find the sword," they vowed. "For Valdoria, and for the world."

Seraphina smiled, a hint of pride in her expression. "I believe in you, Eryndor. But remember, you are not alone in this. The Guardians will support you in any way we can. Take this." She handed Eryndor a small, intricately carved amulet. "This will guide you to the Valley of Echoes. It will light your way when all else seems lost. Trust in it, and trust in yourself."

Eryndor accepted the amulet with a nod of gratitude. They knew that the journey ahead would be long and fraught with danger, but they were ready. The fate of the world depended on the success of their quest, and they would not falter.

With the amulet around their neck and resolve in their heart, Eryndor set out from the stronghold, embarking on the quest that would determine the course of the prophesied battle.

The Journey Begins

THE ROAD TO THE VALLEY of Echoes was long and treacherous, winding through dense forests, across raging rivers, and over towering mountain passes. Eryndor traveled alone, their thoughts their only companion as they made their way deeper into the wilderness. The amulet Seraphina had given them glowed faintly, its light growing stronger as they drew closer to their destination.

Days turned into weeks, and the landscape grew wilder and more desolate. Eryndor encountered many challenges along the way—ravenous beasts that lurked in the shadows, treacherous terrain that threatened to send them tumbling into the abyss, and the ever-present cold that seeped into their bones. But they pressed on, driven by the knowledge that the Sword of Legends was the key to defeating the darkness.

One evening, as the sun dipped below the horizon and the sky turned a deep shade of violet, Eryndor came upon a clearing in the forest. At the center of the clearing stood a massive stone archway, covered in ancient runes that glowed with an ethereal light. The amulet around Eryndor's neck pulsed with energy, confirming that they had reached the first step of their journey.

This was the entrance to the Valley of Echoes, a place spoken of in hushed tones by those who knew of its existence. The valley was said to be a place where the past and present converged, where echoes of long-forgotten battles and ancient heroes lingered in the air. It was a place of great power, but also great danger.

As Eryndor approached the archway, they felt a strange sensation wash over them, as if the very fabric of reality was shifting around them. The air grew heavy, and the light from the setting sun seemed to dim, casting long shadows across the clearing.

Taking a deep breath, Eryndor stepped through the archway and into the Valley of Echoes.

The Valley of Echoes

THE VALLEY OF ECHOES was unlike any place Eryndor had ever seen. The landscape was a surreal blend of jagged peaks, rolling hills, and deep, shadowy ravines. The sky above was a swirling mass of clouds, constantly shifting in color and shape, as if reflecting the ever-changing nature of the valley itself.

But what struck Eryndor the most was the sound. The valley was filled with echoes—whispers, cries, and the clash of steel on steel. These were the echoes of battles fought long ago, of heroes who had come before them, and of the countless souls who had sought the Sword of Legends and failed. The voices of the past swirled around Eryndor, filling their mind with visions of glory and despair, hope and sorrow.

Eryndor knew that the valley was testing them, challenging their resolve. They could feel the weight of the past pressing down on them, the expectations of those who had come before. But they pushed forward, determined to prove themselves worthy.

As they made their way deeper into the valley, the echoes grew louder, more insistent. The landscape shifted around them, the ground beneath their feet seeming to move of its own accord. Eryndor soon realized that the valley was not just a place—it was a living entity, one that was aware of their presence and was testing them at every step.

After hours of navigating the treacherous terrain, Eryndor came to a large stone platform at the center of the valley. At the far end of the platform stood an ancient stone door, covered in intricate carvings and glowing with a faint blue light. Eryndor knew that this was the entrance to the chamber where the Sword of Legends was kept.

But before they could reach the door, a figure appeared on the platform—a tall, imposing figure clad in armor that gleamed in the faint light of the valley. The figure's face was hidden behind a helm, and in its hand, it held a massive sword that pulsed with dark energy.

Eryndor drew their own sword, ready for battle. They knew that this was no ordinary opponent—it was a guardian, a being created to protect the Sword of Legends and to test those who sought to claim it.

The guardian stepped forward, its voice echoing through the valley like a thunderclap. "Who dares seek the Sword of Legends?" it demanded, its tone both commanding and menacing.

"I am Eryndor," they replied, their voice steady. "I seek the Sword of Legends to fulfill the prophecy and to defeat the darkness that threatens the world."

The guardian studied Eryndor for a moment, its eyes glowing with an otherworldly light. "Many have sought the sword before you," it said. "All have failed. The sword is not meant for the weak or the unworthy. If you wish to claim it, you must prove yourself in battle."

Eryndor nodded, their grip on their sword tightening. "I am ready."

The guardian raised its sword, and the two clashed in a battle that shook the very ground beneath them. The guardian's strikes were powerful and precise, each one meant to test Eryndor's strength and skill. But Eryndor fought back with determination, parrying the guardian's blows and countering with swift, calculated strikes of their own.

The battle raged on, the echoes of the valley growing louder with each clash of steel. Eryndor could feel the weight of the past pressing down on them, the expectations of those who had come before. But they refused to let it deter them. They fought with everything they had, drawing on the strength they had gained from their training with the Guardians of the Light.

Finally, with a powerful strike, Eryndor disarmed the guardian, sending its sword clattering to the ground. The guardian stepped back, its form flickering as if it were fading from existence.

"You have proven yourself worthy," the guardian said, its voice now softer, almost reverent. "The Sword of Legends awaits you. But remember this—your journey is far from over. The sword is a tool, a symbol of your strength, but it is not the source of your power. That power lies within you, Eryndor. Never forget that."

With those words, the guardian vanished, leaving Eryndor alone on the platform. The stone door at the far end of the platform began to open, revealing a staircase that led down into the depths of the valley.

Eryndor sheathed their sword and took a deep breath. The battle had been fierce, but they had emerged victorious. Now, they had to descend into the chamber below and claim the Sword of Legends.

The Chamber of Trials

THE STAIRCASE LED ERYNDOR deep into the heart of the valley, the air growing colder and heavier with each step. The echoes of the past still filled their ears, but now, they were joined by a new sound—a low, rhythmic thrum that seemed to resonate through the very walls of the chamber.

Finally, after what felt like an eternity, Eryndor reached the bottom of the staircase and stepped into a massive chamber. The chamber was dimly lit by the faint blue light that emanated from the walls, casting eerie shadows across the floor. At the center of the chamber stood a stone pedestal, and resting atop it was the Sword of Legends.

The sword was magnificent, its blade gleaming with an otherworldly light. The hilt was intricately designed, with runes and symbols that glowed faintly in the darkness. It was a weapon of immense power, one that had been forged in the fires of the ancient world and blessed by the gods themselves.

But as Eryndor approached the pedestal, they felt a sudden surge of energy in the air. The echoes that had filled the valley now grew louder, more intense, and the chamber itself seemed to come alive with power.

Before Eryndor could reach the sword, three figures materialized in the chamber, each one glowing with a different light—one blue, one red, and one green. These were the ancient guardians of the Sword of Legends, the final test that Eryndor would have to face before they could claim the weapon.

The first guardian, glowing blue, stepped forward and spoke. "The Sword of Legends is a weapon of great power, but it is also a weapon of great responsibility. You must prove that you possess the wisdom to wield it. Answer this riddle, and you may proceed."

Eryndor nodded, ready for the challenge.

The blue guardian recited the riddle: "I speak without a mouth and hear without ears. I have no body, but I come alive with the wind. What am I?"

Eryndor considered the riddle carefully. It was a test of their intellect, meant to determine if they were worthy of wielding the sword. After a moment, they smiled, confident in their answer.

"You are an echo," Eryndor replied.

The blue guardian nodded in approval and stepped back, allowing the second guardian, glowing red, to step forward.

"The Sword of Legends is not just a weapon—it is a symbol of courage," the red guardian said. "To claim it, you must face your deepest fears. Look into the flames and confront what lies within."

As the red guardian spoke, a ring of fire erupted around Eryndor, encircling them in its intense heat. Within the flames, Eryndor saw visions—visions of the battle to come, of the darkness that threatened to consume the world, and of the lives that would be lost if they failed.

But the flames also showed Eryndor something else—visions of their own fears and doubts. They saw themselves standing alone on a battlefield, surrounded by enemies, their friends and allies lying dead at their feet. They saw themselves faltering in the face of overwhelming odds, succumbing to the darkness that sought to destroy them.

Eryndor's heart pounded in their chest as the flames grew higher, the visions more intense. But they refused to give in to fear. They had come too far, faced too many challenges to let doubt stop them now.

Drawing on the strength they had gained from their training and the support of the Guardians, Eryndor stepped forward, walking through the flames and emerging unscathed. The visions faded, and the flames died down, leaving Eryndor standing tall, their resolve stronger than ever.

The red guardian nodded in approval and stepped back, allowing the third and final guardian, glowing green, to step forward.

"The Sword of Legends is a weapon of strength, but true strength is not just physical," the green guardian said. "To claim it, you must demonstrate your inner strength, your resolve to see this quest through to the end, no matter the cost."

With those words, the green guardian raised its hand, and the chamber began to tremble. The walls cracked, and the floor beneath Eryndor's feet shifted, threatening to collapse. The amulet around Eryndor's neck glowed brightly, but the path to the sword was blocked by a massive chasm that had opened in the center of the chamber.

Eryndor knew that this was the final test—a test of their willpower and determination. The chasm before them was wide and deep, and crossing it would require not just physical strength, but also courage and trust in themselves.

Taking a deep breath, Eryndor focused on the amulet's light and prepared to make the leap. They knew that this was a test not just of their ability to reach the sword, but of their faith in their own abilities.

With a burst of energy, Eryndor leaped across the chasm, the amulet guiding their way. For a moment, it seemed as if they would fall into the abyss, but at the last moment, they landed safely on the other side, the sword just within reach.

The green guardian nodded in approval and vanished, leaving Eryndor alone in the chamber once more. The echoes had faded, and the chamber was silent, save for the faint thrum of energy that pulsed from the Sword of Legends.

With a sense of reverence, Eryndor approached the pedestal and reached out to take the sword. As their hand closed around the hilt, they felt a surge of power flow through them, filling them with a strength and resolve they had never known before.

The Sword of Legends was theirs.

The Return

WITH THE SWORD OF LEGENDS in hand, Eryndor made their way out of the Valley of Echoes, retracing their steps through the treacherous landscape. But now, the journey seemed easier, as if the sword itself was guiding them, lighting their path and clearing the obstacles that had once seemed insurmountable.

The echoes of the valley were still present, but now, they seemed to sing a different song—a song of triumph and hope, of victory over darkness. Eryndor could feel the power of the sword coursing through them, and they knew that they were ready for the battle to come.

When Eryndor finally emerged from the valley, they were greeted by the Guardians of the Light, who had been waiting for their return. Seraphina stepped forward, her eyes filled with pride as she saw the sword in Eryndor's hand.

"You have done well, Eryndor," Seraphina said, her voice filled with emotion. "The Sword of Legends is a symbol of your strength, your courage, and your determination. With this weapon, you have the power to fulfill the prophecy and to lead us to victory."

Eryndor nodded, their heart swelling with a sense of purpose. "The sword is powerful, but it is not the source of my strength. That strength comes from within—from the belief that we can overcome the darkness, no matter the cost."

Seraphina smiled, a tear glistening in her eye. "You have truly become the hero the prophecy spoke of, Eryndor. The world may tremble, but with you leading the way, I know that we will prevail."

With the Sword of Legends in hand and the Guardians by their side, Eryndor returned to the stronghold, ready to face the darkness that threatened to consume the world. The journey had been long and difficult, but it had also been a journey of growth, of discovery, and of transformation.

The Sword of Legends was more than just a weapon—it was a symbol of hope, of the light that could overcome even the deepest darkness. And as Eryndor prepared for the battle to come, they knew that they were ready to fulfill their destiny, to lead the forces of light against the darkness, and to alter the course of the prophesied battle.

The storm was gathering, the darkness rising, but with the Sword of Legends in their hand and the strength of their resolve in their heart, Eryndor was ready to face whatever challenges lay ahead.

The hero had returned, and the world would never be the same.

End of Chapter 4

Chapter 5: The Warriors of the Fallen

The Origins of the Fallen

In the annals of Valdorian history, there were tales of a group of warriors whose deeds were whispered in the same breath as legends. These were not the stories of noble knights or celebrated heroes, but of those who had been broken by tragedy, who had lost everything and yet found within themselves the strength to rise again. They were known as the Fallen—a band of elite warriors bound together by their shared pain and driven by an unyielding desire for redemption.

The Fallen were not a formal order, nor were they bound by oaths of loyalty to a single kingdom or cause. Instead, they were brought together by fate, their paths converging as the world teetered on the brink of darkness. Each member of the Fallen had suffered a great loss—some had lost loved ones, others had seen their homes destroyed, and still others had been betrayed by those they once trusted. But in the face of such overwhelming despair, they had chosen not to succumb, but to fight.

The prophecy of blood spoke of a great battle, one that would determine the fate of the world. And as the signs of the prophecy grew more pronounced, the Fallen began to sense that their time had come. They had been forged in the fires of their own suffering, and now, they would bring that fire to bear against the darkness that threatened to consume all they held dear.

But the path to redemption was not an easy one. Each of the Fallen carried with them the weight of their past, the scars of their losses, and the memories of the lives they had left behind. And yet, it was these very scars that made them who they were—warriors of unparalleled skill and determination, willing to do whatever it took to protect the world from the encroaching darkness.

The Gathering of the Fallen

AS THE WORLD PREPARED for the prophesied battle, Eryndor knew that they could not face the darkness alone. The Sword of Legends was a powerful weapon, but it was not enough. They needed allies—warriors who understood the stakes, who had faced the darkness in their own lives and emerged stronger for it. And so, Eryndor set out to find the Fallen, to bring together a group of warriors who would stand with them in the battle to come.

The first of the Fallen that Eryndor sought was a man known as Kael the Unbroken. Kael was a giant of a man, with broad shoulders and arms as thick as tree trunks. His face was scarred from countless battles, and his eyes held the haunted look of someone who had seen too much. Kael had once been the commander of a great army, but his life had been shattered when his homeland was invaded and his family slaughtered before his eyes. He had wandered the world ever since, fighting in one battle after another, searching for a way to numb the pain of his loss.

Eryndor found Kael in a small village at the edge of the kingdom, where he had taken up the life of a blacksmith. But even here, far from the battlefields of his past, the ghosts of his family haunted him. When Eryndor approached Kael and told him of the prophecy and the battle that was to come, Kael at first refused to listen. He was tired, he said, tired of fighting, tired of losing, tired of the endless cycle of violence and death.

But Eryndor saw something in Kael—something that had not been extinguished, despite all he had been through. They spoke to him of redemption, of the chance to fight not for revenge, but for something greater. They spoke of the Sword of Legends, and of the hope that it could bring to a world on the brink of destruction.

In the end, it was not Eryndor's words that convinced Kael to join the fight, but the memory of his family. He knew that he could never bring them back, but perhaps, by fighting alongside Eryndor, he could prevent others from suffering the same fate. Kael the Unbroken joined the ranks of the Fallen, and with him came the strength and experience of a lifetime of war.

The next warrior Eryndor sought was a woman known as Lyra the Shadowblade. Lyra was a master of stealth and assassination, her movements as silent as the night, her strikes as deadly as the bite of a viper. She had once been a member of the Umbrosian assassins' guild, trained from a young age to be a weapon in the service of the Shadow Council. But Lyra had turned her back on her masters after they betrayed her, sending her on a mission that led to the death of her only sister.

Consumed by grief and guilt, Lyra had fled the guild, becoming a shadow in the night, a rogue assassin who took on only the most dangerous contracts. Her reputation was legendary—no target had ever escaped her blade, no matter how well-guarded. But despite her skills, Lyra was haunted by the memory of her sister, and by the knowledge that she had been used as a pawn by those she had once trusted.

Eryndor found Lyra in a dark corner of the city of Umbra, where she was preparing to carry out her latest contract. At first, she was wary of Eryndor, suspicious of their intentions. But as they spoke, Eryndor revealed the truth of the prophecy and the battle that was to come. They told Lyra that she was not alone in her pain, that others had suffered as she had, and that together, they could fight to bring an end to the darkness that had consumed their lives.

Lyra was silent for a long time, her mind racing as she considered Eryndor's words. She had spent so long in the shadows, alone and mistrustful, that the idea of fighting for something greater seemed almost foreign to her. But in the end, it was the thought of her sister that convinced her. Lyra had vowed to never again allow herself to be used as a tool by others, but she also knew that she could not continue to live in the shadows forever. Perhaps, by joining Eryndor, she could find a way to honor her sister's memory and bring some measure of peace to her own troubled soul.

And so, Lyra the Shadowblade joined the ranks of the Fallen, bringing with her the skills of an assassin and the determination of a woman seeking redemption.

The third warrior Eryndor sought was a man known as Torin the Flameborn. Torin was a sorcerer of great power, his mastery of fire magic unparalleled in the land. But Torin's life had been marked by tragedy—his village had been destroyed in a magical accident when he was just a child, and he had been the only survivor. The flames that had consumed his home had also scarred him, leaving him with burns that covered much of his body and a deep fear of the power he wielded.

Despite his fear, Torin had trained as a sorcerer, determined to control the power that had once nearly destroyed him. But his fear never left him, and it was this fear that had led him to isolate himself from others, retreating to a remote tower where he could practice his magic in solitude. He had spent years trying to master his powers, but no matter how much he trained, the fear of losing control always lingered in the back of his mind.

Eryndor found Torin in his tower, surrounded by books and scrolls, his face half-hidden in the shadows. At first, Torin refused to even speak to Eryndor, convinced that they were just another distraction from his training. But Eryndor persisted, telling Torin of the prophecy and the battle that was to come. They spoke of the power of the Sword of Legends, and how it could be used to bring an end to the darkness that threatened the world.

Torin listened, his interest piqued despite himself. He had always believed that his powers were a curse, something to be feared and controlled. But as Eryndor spoke, he began to wonder if perhaps his powers could be used for something greater. Perhaps, by fighting alongside Eryndor, he could find a way to overcome his fear and finally come to terms with the power that had haunted him for so long.

And so, Torin the Flameborn joined the ranks of the Fallen, bringing with him the power of fire and the determination to overcome his own fears.

The final warrior Eryndor sought was a woman known as Elara the Starseer. Elara was a seer, gifted with the ability to see into the future and to glimpse the threads of fate that wove through the world. But Elara's gift had also been her curse—her visions had shown her the deaths of those she loved, and no matter how hard she tried, she could not change their fates. Her family had perished in a plague that swept through her village, and Elara had been left alone, haunted by the knowledge that she had seen their deaths before they had occurred and had been powerless to stop them.

Elara had wandered the land since then, using her gift to help others where she could, but always keeping her distance, afraid of forming attachments that might lead to more pain. She had become known as the Starseer, a mysterious figure who appeared in times of crisis and offered guidance to those in need.

Eryndor found Elara in a small village on the edge of the kingdom, where she had been helping the villagers prepare for the coming winter. At first, Elara was reluctant to join Eryndor, fearful of what her visions might show her. But as they spoke, Eryndor told Elara of the prophecy and the battle that was to come. They spoke of the power of the Sword of Legends, and how it could be used to alter the course of fate itself.

Elara was intrigued, but also wary. She had spent so long trying to avoid the pain of loss, but now she was being asked to join a fight that would almost certainly bring more suffering. But as Eryndor spoke, Elara began to see a glimmer of hope. Perhaps, by fighting alongside Eryndor and the other Fallen, she could find a way to change the future, to prevent the darkness from consuming the world.

And so, Elara the Starseer joined the ranks of the Fallen, bringing with her the gift of foresight and the hope of altering the course of fate.

The Trials of the Fallen

WITH THE FALLEN ASSEMBLED, Eryndor knew that their journey was far from over. The prophecy spoke of a great battle, but it did not say when or where it would take place. The world was still on the brink of darkness, and the forces of evil were growing stronger with each passing day. The Fallen would need to train, to hone their skills and to learn to work together as a team if they were to stand a chance against the darkness.

The Guardians of the Light welcomed the Fallen into their stronghold, offering them a place to train and prepare for the battle to come. Each member of the Fallen was skilled in their own right, but they had all spent so long fighting alone that it took time for them to learn to trust one another, to rely on each other's strengths and to support each other's weaknesses.

Kael the Unbroken trained with the Guardians' master-at-arms, honing his already formidable combat skills and learning new techniques that would help him in the battle to come. But Kael's true challenge was not physical—it was emotional. He had spent so long burying his pain beneath a facade of strength that he struggled to open up to the other members of the Fallen, to share his burden and to accept their support.

Lyra the Shadowblade trained in the art of stealth and assassination, perfecting her already deadly skills and learning new techniques that would allow her to strike from the shadows and eliminate her enemies before they even knew she was there. But Lyra's true challenge was not one of skill—it was one of trust. She had spent so long living in the shadows, mistrusting everyone around her, that she struggled to let down her guard and to rely on the other members of the Fallen.

Torin the Flameborn trained in the use of his fire magic, learning new spells and techniques that would allow him to control his power and to use it to devastating effect in battle. But Torin's true challenge was not one of magic—it was one of fear. He had spent so long fearing his own power, afraid of losing control and causing harm, that he struggled to embrace his abilities and to see them as a gift rather than a curse.

Elara the Starseer trained in the use of her gift of foresight, learning to control her visions and to use them to guide the Fallen in their quest. But Elara's true challenge was not one of foresight—it was one of acceptance. She had spent so long trying to avoid the pain of loss, afraid of forming attachments that might lead to more suffering, that she struggled to open her heart to the other members of the Fallen and to accept that loss was a part of life.

Eryndor trained alongside the Fallen, honing their skills with the Sword of Legends and learning new techniques that would allow them to lead the Fallen in battle. But Eryndor's true challenge was not one of leadership—it was one of responsibility. They had spent so long focused on their own quest, on their own destiny, that they struggled to accept the responsibility of leading others and to see the Fallen not just as allies, but as friends.

As the weeks passed, the Fallen began to grow closer, forming bonds that were forged in the fires of their shared pain and their shared determination to fight the darkness. They trained together, fought together, and learned to rely on each other in ways that they had never relied on anyone before. They shared their stories, their losses, and their hopes for the future, and in doing so, they began to heal the wounds of their pasts.

But even as they grew stronger as a team, the darkness continued to gather. The signs of the prophecy were growing more pronounced, and the world was on the brink of war. The time for training was coming to an end, and the time for battle was drawing near.

The First Battle

THE DAY OF THE FIRST battle dawned cold and gray, the sky heavy with the promise of rain. The Fallen stood on the battlements of the Guardians' stronghold, looking out over the valley below. The forces of darkness had gathered, their numbers vast and their intentions clear. They had come for the Sword of Legends, for Eryndor, and for the Fallen.

Eryndor stood at the forefront, the Sword of Legends gleaming in their hand. They could feel the power of the sword coursing through them, filling them with a strength and determination that they had never known before. But they also knew that this battle would not be won by the sword alone. It would be won by the strength of the Fallen, by their determination to fight for what they had lost and for the future they hoped to build.

Kael the Unbroken stood beside Eryndor, his massive warhammer slung across his back. He had faced countless battles in his life, but this one was different. This one was not just about survival—it was about redemption. Kael knew that he could never bring back his family, but perhaps, by fighting in this battle, he could find some measure of peace.

Lyra the Shadowblade crouched in the shadows, her twin daggers gleaming in the dim light. She had spent so long living in the darkness, fighting alone, that the idea of fighting alongside others was still foreign to her. But Lyra had come to trust the Fallen, to rely on them in ways that she had never relied on anyone before. She knew that this battle would test her in ways that she had never been tested before, but she was ready.

Torin the Flameborn stood at the rear, his hands glowing with the power of fire. He had spent so long fearing his own power, afraid of losing control, that the idea of using it in battle was both exhilarating and terrifying. But Torin had come to see his power not as a curse, but as a gift. He knew that this battle would be his chance to prove that he could control his power, that he could use it for something greater than himself.

Elara the Starseer stood beside Torin, her eyes closed as she focused on her visions. She had spent so long trying to avoid the pain of loss, afraid of forming attachments that might lead to more suffering, that the idea of fighting alongside the Fallen was both comforting and terrifying. But Elara had come to see the Fallen not just as allies, but as friends. She knew that this battle would test her in ways that she had never been tested before, but she was ready.

As the forces of darkness advanced, the Fallen prepared for battle. They knew that this would be the first of many battles, that the war was just beginning, but they were ready. They had been forged in the fires of their own suffering, and now they would bring that fire to bear against the darkness that threatened to consume the world.

The battle was fierce and brutal, the forces of darkness relentless in their assault. The Fallen fought with everything they had, their skills and determination pushing them to the limits of their abilities. Kael's warhammer crushed through the ranks of the enemy, Lyra's daggers struck from the shadows with deadly precision, Torin's fire magic engulfed the battlefield in flames, and Elara's visions guided the Fallen's movements, helping them to anticipate and counter the enemy's attacks.

Eryndor fought at the forefront, the Sword of Legends cutting through the enemy like a beacon of light in the darkness. But even with the sword's power, the battle was far from easy. The forces of darkness were vast and powerful, their numbers seemingly endless. But the Fallen did not falter. They fought with the strength of those who had lost everything, with the determination of those who sought redemption through victory.

As the battle raged on, the sky darkened, and a storm began to brew. Lightning flashed across the sky, and the wind howled through the valley. But even as the storm raged, the Fallen continued to fight, their resolve unwavering.

Finally, after what felt like an eternity, the forces of darkness began to retreat. The Fallen had won the day, but they knew that the battle was far from over. The darkness would return, stronger and more determined than ever. But the Fallen were ready. They had faced their first test, and they had emerged victorious.

As the storm began to abate, the Fallen stood together on the battlefield, their faces grim but determined. They had won the battle, but the war was just beginning. The prophecy of blood was still unfolding, and the forces of darkness were still gathering. But the Fallen knew that they would not face the darkness alone. They had each other, and they had Eryndor, the chosen one who would lead them to victory.

The storm had gathered, the darkness had risen, but the Fallen had stood their ground. They were warriors of the fallen, bound together by their shared pain and their shared determination to fight for a better future. And as they prepared for the battles to come, they knew that they would face whatever challenges lay ahead with courage, strength, and the unwavering belief that they could overcome even the deepest darkness.

End of Chapter 5

Chapter 6: The Siege of the Dark Fortress

The Fortress of Shadows

High atop a jagged mountain range, hidden from the eyes of those who dwelled in the sunlit lands, stood the Dark Fortress. Its towering spires pierced the stormy sky, and its blackened walls loomed like a shadow over the world below. This was the stronghold of the enemy, a place where darkness thrived and where the forces of evil gathered to plot the downfall of the kingdoms of light.

The Dark Fortress had long been a symbol of fear, its very name whispered in dread by those who knew of its existence. Legends told of the horrors that lurked within its walls—creatures born of shadow, dark sorcerers who wielded forbidden magic, and armies of the undead, bound to serve their malevolent masters. But the fortress was more than just a place of terror; it was the heart of the enemy's power, the center of the darkness that threatened to engulf the world.

For years, the location of the Dark Fortress had been a mystery, its existence known only to a select few. But as the signs of the prophecy of blood grew more pronounced, the forces of light had begun to uncover the truth. Scouts and spies had risked their lives to gather information, and their efforts had finally borne fruit. The location of the Dark Fortress had been revealed, and with it, the opportunity to strike at the heart of the enemy's power.

The decision to lay siege to the Dark Fortress had not been made lightly. The forces of light knew that the battle would be fierce, and that the cost would be high. But they also knew that they could not allow the darkness to continue to spread unchecked. The time had come to take the fight to the enemy, to challenge the forces of evil on their own ground.

And so, the armies of light began to gather, their banners fluttering in the wind as they marched toward the Dark Fortress. At their head was Eryndor, the Chosen One, bearing the Sword of Legends and the weight of the prophecy on their shoulders. This would be their first major conflict as a leader, and they knew that the outcome of the siege would set the tone for the battles to come.

The Forces of Light Assemble

THE JOURNEY TO THE Dark Fortress was long and perilous, the path winding through treacherous mountains and dense forests where the shadows seemed to cling to the very air. The forces of light moved with caution, their scouts constantly on the lookout for signs of the enemy. They knew that the darkness had many eyes, and that their approach would not go unnoticed.

As the armies of light made their way toward the fortress, they were joined by reinforcements from the neighboring kingdoms. Eloria, Drakoria, Thaloria, and even Umbrosia had sent their best warriors to join the fight, united by the common threat of the darkness that sought to consume them all. The alliance was fragile, born of necessity rather than trust, but it was the only hope they had of standing against the enemy.

The camp of the forces of light stretched for miles across the valley at the base of the mountain where the Dark Fortress stood. Tents were pitched, fires were lit, and the sound of preparations for battle filled the air. Soldiers sharpened their swords, archers strung their bows, and mages prepared their spells, all knowing that the coming battle would be unlike any they had ever faced.

Eryndor moved among the troops, speaking words of encouragement and reassurance. They could see the fear in the eyes of the soldiers, the uncertainty that lingered beneath their resolve. Many of these men and women had never faced the kind of darkness that awaited them within the walls of the Dark Fortress. But Eryndor knew that fear was a natural part of battle, and that it could be overcome with courage and determination.

As Eryndor walked through the camp, they were joined by the Fallen—Kael the Unbroken, Lyra the Shadowblade, Torin the Flameborn, and Elara the Starseer. Each of the Fallen had taken on a leadership role within the army, their unique skills and experience invaluable in the preparation for the siege.

"The troops are ready," Kael reported, his voice steady and confident. "They know what's at stake, and they're prepared to fight."

"The scouts have reported increased activity within the fortress," Lyra added, her eyes narrowing as she spoke. "The enemy knows we're coming. They'll be ready for us."

Torin nodded in agreement. "The magic within the fortress is strong, but we've prepared countermeasures. The mages are confident they can neutralize the enemy's defenses."

Eryndor listened to their reports, their mind racing as they considered the strategy for the siege. The Dark Fortress was a formidable stronghold, and the enemy within was powerful. But Eryndor knew that they could not afford to hesitate. The forces of light had come this far, and they would not turn back now.

"The time has come," Eryndor said, their voice filled with determination. "We will lay siege to the Dark Fortress at dawn. We will strike with all the strength we have, and we will not stop until the enemy is defeated."

The Fallen nodded in agreement, their expressions grim but resolute. They knew that the battle ahead would be fierce, but they were ready to face whatever challenges lay ahead. Together with Eryndor, they would lead the forces of light in the first major conflict of the prophecy, a battle that would determine the course of the war.

The Siege Begins

AS THE FIRST LIGHT of dawn broke over the mountains, the forces of light began their advance toward the Dark Fortress. The sound of marching feet echoed through the valley, the air filled with the tension of impending battle. The soldiers moved with purpose, their hearts steeled for the fight that lay ahead.

The Dark Fortress loomed before them, its blackened walls towering above the landscape. The fortress was an imposing sight, a bastion of darkness that seemed to defy the very light of the sun. The spires of the fortress were wreathed in shadow, and the air around it crackled with dark energy. It was a place of evil, and it radiated a malevolent power that sent a chill down the spine of even the bravest warrior.

As the forces of light approached the fortress, the enemy began to reveal themselves. The gates of the fortress creaked open, and from within poured an army of darkness—legions of undead warriors, twisted creatures born of shadow, and dark sorcerers who wielded forbidden magic. The enemy was vast and powerful, their numbers seemingly endless, but the forces of light were undeterred.

Eryndor raised the Sword of Legends high, the blade gleaming with a brilliant light that cut through the darkness. "For the light!" they cried, their voice carrying across the battlefield.

"For the light!" the soldiers echoed, their voices rising in a chorus of defiance.

The battle began with a thunderous clash as the two armies met in the shadow of the Dark Fortress. Swords clashed against shields, arrows whistled through the air, and the ground shook with the force of the combatants. The forces of light fought with everything they had, their resolve unyielding in the face of the overwhelming darkness.

Kael the Unbroken led the charge, his massive warhammer smashing through the ranks of the enemy with relentless force. He fought with the strength of a man who had lost everything and had nothing left to lose. Each strike of his hammer sent shockwaves through the battlefield, and the enemy fell before him like wheat before the scythe.

Lyra the Shadowblade moved through the battlefield like a wraith, her twin daggers flashing in the dim light. She struck from the shadows, her blades finding the weak points in the enemy's armor and felling them with deadly precision. She was a whirlwind of death, her movements fluid and graceful as she danced through the ranks of the enemy.

Torin the Flameborn stood at the rear, his hands glowing with the power of fire. He unleashed waves of flame upon the enemy, his magic engulfing the battlefield in a sea of fire. The dark sorcerers who opposed him were powerful, but Torin's mastery of fire magic was unmatched. He fought with the determination of a man who had finally come to terms with his own power, and the flames he wielded were a reflection of the fire that burned within his heart.

Elara the Starseer used her gift of foresight to guide the forces of light, her visions allowing her to anticipate the enemy's movements and to warn her allies of impending danger. She was a beacon of hope on the battlefield, her calm presence and wise counsel giving the soldiers the strength to continue fighting even when the odds seemed insurmountable.

Eryndor fought at the forefront, the Sword of Legends cutting through the enemy with a brilliance that lit up the battlefield. The sword's power was immense, its light searing through the darkness and weakening the enemy's defenses. But even with the sword's power, Eryndor knew that they could not win the battle alone. They needed the strength and support of the Fallen, of the soldiers who fought beside them, and of the allies who had joined them in the fight.

The siege of the Dark Fortress raged on for hours, the forces of light slowly pushing their way toward the gates of the fortress. The casualties were heavy on both sides, the ground littered with the bodies of the fallen. But the forces of light did not falter. They fought with the knowledge that this battle was just the beginning, that the fate of the world depended on their victory.

As the sun began to rise higher in the sky, casting its light over the battlefield, Eryndor knew that the time had come to make their move. They had fought their way to the gates of the fortress, and now they needed to breach its walls and bring the fight to the heart of the enemy's power.

"Kael, Lyra, Torin, Elara!" Eryndor called out, their voice carrying over the sounds of battle. "We need to breach the gates! This is our chance to strike at the heart of the darkness!"

The Fallen responded without hesitation, rallying their forces and focusing their efforts on the gates of the fortress. Kael led the charge, his warhammer smashing against the gates with the force of a battering ram. Lyra moved through the shadows, picking off the enemy archers who sought to defend the gates. Torin unleashed a torrent of fire, weakening the gate's defenses, while Elara used her visions to guide the soldiers and to counter the dark magic that protected the fortress.

The gates groaned under the assault, the ancient wood and metal cracking and splintering under the combined might of the Fallen. The enemy fought desperately to hold the gates, but the forces of light were relentless. Finally, with a resounding crash, the gates gave way, and the forces of light surged forward, pouring into the fortress with a fury born of righteous determination.

The Battle Within

THE INTERIOR OF THE Dark Fortress was a labyrinth of twisted corridors, dark chambers, and hidden traps. The forces of light moved cautiously through the fortress, their senses heightened as they prepared for the enemy's next move. The darkness within the fortress was oppressive, the air thick with malevolent energy that seemed to sap the strength of those who entered.

Eryndor led the way, the Sword of Legends lighting their path through the darkness. The fortress was vast, its halls echoing with the sounds of battle as the forces of light clashed with the enemy at every turn. The corridors were narrow and winding, the walls lined with ancient carvings and symbols of dark power. It was a place of evil, a place where the forces of darkness had gathered to plot the downfall of the world.

The further the forces of light advanced into the fortress, the more intense the resistance became. The enemy had fortified their positions, using the narrow corridors and tight spaces to their advantage. But the forces of light were determined, their resolve unshaken by the enemy's efforts to halt their advance.

Kael fought with relentless determination, his warhammer smashing through the enemy's defenses with brutal force. He led the charge through the narrow corridors, his presence a rallying point for the soldiers who followed him. Kael's strength and leadership were crucial in the confined spaces of the fortress, where every inch of ground gained was hard-fought.

Lyra moved through the shadows, her daggers finding their mark with deadly precision. She used the labyrinthine corridors of the fortress to her advantage, slipping through the enemy's defenses and striking from behind. Lyra's skills as an assassin were invaluable in the close-quarters combat of the fortress, where speed and precision were key.

Torin used his fire magic to clear the way for the forces of light, his flames illuminating the darkness and burning through the enemy's defenses. The confined spaces of the fortress made his fire magic all the more devastating, the heat and flames forcing the enemy to retreat or be consumed by the inferno.

Torin fought with a confidence and control that he had never known before, his fear of his own power finally giving way to the realization that he could use it to protect those he cared about.

Elara used her visions to guide the forces of light through the maze-like corridors of the fortress, her foresight allowing her to anticipate the enemy's traps and to warn her allies of impending danger. She was a calming presence amidst the chaos of battle, her wisdom and insight helping the soldiers to stay focused and to press forward despite the odds.

As the forces of light advanced deeper into the fortress, they encountered the heart of the enemy's power—a massive chamber at the center of the fortress, where the dark sorcerers had gathered to conduct their forbidden rituals. The chamber was filled with dark energy, the air crackling with malevolent power. At the center of the chamber stood a massive stone altar, upon which lay a dark crystal that pulsed with a sinister light.

The dark sorcerers had been preparing for this moment, channeling their magic into the crystal to summon forth the full power of the darkness. But the forces of light had arrived before the ritual could be completed, and now, the sorcerers stood ready to defend their stronghold.

Eryndor knew that this was the moment of truth. The dark crystal was the source of the enemy's power, and if they could destroy it, they could weaken the darkness and turn the tide of the battle. But the sorcerers were powerful, and the chamber was heavily fortified. It would take all of their strength, all of their skill, to succeed.

"We have to destroy the crystal," Eryndor said, their voice filled with urgency. "If we can do that, we can weaken the darkness and break the enemy's hold on the fortress."

The Fallen nodded in agreement, their expressions grim but determined. They knew that this was the moment they had been preparing for, the moment that would determine the outcome of the siege.

Kael led the charge into the chamber, his warhammer smashing through the ranks of the dark sorcerers with brutal force. Lyra moved through the shadows, her daggers striking down the sorcerers who sought to protect the crystal. Torin unleashed a torrent of fire, engulfing the chamber in flames and disrupting the sorcerers' rituals. Elara used her visions to guide the forces of light, helping them to avoid the enemy's traps and to focus their efforts on the crystal.

Eryndor fought at the forefront, the Sword of Legends blazing with a light that cut through the darkness. The dark sorcerers were powerful, their magic formidable, but Eryndor's resolve was unshakable. They knew that they had to destroy the crystal, no matter the cost.

The battle in the chamber was fierce, the forces of light and darkness clashing in a struggle for control. The dark sorcerers fought with everything they had, their magic lashing out with deadly force. But the forces of light were relentless, their determination unyielding.

Finally, after what felt like an eternity, Eryndor reached the altar. The dark crystal pulsed with malevolent energy, its power threatening to overwhelm them. But Eryndor knew that this was the moment of truth, the moment that would determine the fate of the siege.

With a cry of defiance, Eryndor raised the Sword of Legends high and brought it down upon the crystal. The blade struck with a resounding crash, and the crystal shattered into a thousand pieces. A wave of dark energy exploded from the crystal, sweeping through the chamber and shaking the very foundations of the fortress.

The dark sorcerers cried out in despair as the crystal was destroyed, their power weakened and their hold on the fortress broken. The forces of light surged forward, overwhelming the remaining defenders and securing the chamber.

The Siege of the Dark Fortress had been won.

The Aftermath

AS THE DUST SETTLED and the last echoes of battle faded, the forces of light stood victorious in the heart of the Dark Fortress. The enemy had been defeated, their power broken, and the fortress had been secured. But the cost had been high, and the battlefield was littered with the bodies of the fallen.

Eryndor stood in the shattered remains of the chamber, the Sword of Legends still glowing with a faint light. They were exhausted, their body battered and bruised from the battle, but their heart was filled with a sense of triumph. The siege had been their first major conflict as a leader, and they had emerged victorious.

The Fallen gathered around Eryndor, their faces etched with exhaustion but also with pride. They had fought together, faced the darkness together, and they had won. The bonds they had forged in battle were stronger than ever, and they knew that they would need that strength in the battles to come.

Kael placed a hand on Eryndor's shoulder, his voice filled with respect. "You led us well, Eryndor. We couldn't have done this without you."

Lyra nodded in agreement, a rare smile crossing her face. "The darkness won't go down easily, but today, we showed them what we're made of."

Torin looked around at the chamber, the remnants of the dark crystal still glowing faintly. "We've weakened their power, but the darkness is far from defeated. We'll need to stay vigilant."

Elara closed her eyes, her visions showing her glimpses of the future. "The road ahead is still long, but today we took the first step. The light will prevail, as long as we stand together."

Eryndor looked at their friends, their allies, and felt a sense of gratitude and determination. They knew that the Siege of the Dark Fortress was just the beginning, that the prophecy was still unfolding, and that the battles to come would be even more challenging. But they also knew that they were not alone, that they had the strength and support of the Fallen and the forces of light.

As the forces of light began to tend to the wounded and to prepare for the next phase of their campaign, Eryndor felt a renewed sense of purpose. They had proven themselves as a leader, but more importantly, they had proven that the light could stand against the darkness.

The Siege of the Dark Fortress would go down in history as the first major victory in the war against the darkness, a turning point in the battle to save the world. But Eryndor knew that the war was far from over. The forces of darkness would regroup, and the prophecy would continue to unfold.

But with the Sword of Legends in their hand and the strength of the Fallen by their side

, Eryndor was ready to face whatever challenges lay ahead. The siege had been won, but the true battle was just beginning.

The light had triumphed, but the war was far from over.

End of Chapter 6

Chapter 7: The Betrayal Within

The Aftermath of Victory

The victory at the Dark Fortress had been hard-won, but it had also been a moment of triumph for the forces of light. The fortress, once a bastion of darkness, had fallen, and the enemy's power had been significantly weakened. The soldiers who had survived the siege were weary but proud, their spirits lifted by the knowledge that they had struck a decisive blow against the forces of evil.

Eryndor stood at the edge of the fortress's battlements, looking out over the vast landscape that stretched below. The sky was clear, the storm that had raged during the battle now gone, leaving behind a sense of calm that belied the horrors that had taken place just hours before. The Sword of Legends hung at Eryndor's side, its light dimmed now that the immediate threat had been vanquished, but its presence was still a comfort—a reminder of the power they wielded and the responsibility that came with it.

The Fallen were scattered throughout the fortress, each tending to the tasks that had fallen to them in the aftermath of the battle. Kael the Unbroken was overseeing the fortification of the fortress's defenses, ensuring that it would not fall back into enemy hands. Lyra the Shadowblade was patrolling the perimeter, her keen eyes and sharp instincts on high alert for any signs of a counterattack. Torin the Flameborn was working with the mages to cleanse the fortress of the dark magic that still lingered within its walls. Elara the Starseer was tending to the wounded, using her foresight to guide the healers in their work.

But even as the forces of light began to settle into their victory, a sense of unease lingered in the air. The battle had been won, but the war was far from over. The enemy was still out there, regrouping, and preparing to strike again.

And there were other dangers as well—dangers that could not be seen or fought with swords and magic.

Eryndor knew that they could not afford to let their guard down. The victory at the Dark Fortress had been crucial, but it had also made them a target. The enemy would not rest until they had reclaimed what they had lost, and Eryndor suspected that the next attack would come from a direction they did not expect.

As Eryndor descended from the battlements and made their way through the fortress, they could not shake the feeling that something was wrong. The air felt heavy, charged with a tension that had not been there before. The soldiers they passed seemed on edge, their conversations hushed and their eyes filled with uncertainty. It was as if the fortress itself was holding its breath, waiting for something to happen.

And then it did.

The First Signs

IT BEGAN WITH WHISPERS—SMALL, insidious rumors that spread like wildfire through the ranks of the soldiers. No one knew exactly where they had come from or who had started them, but they quickly took root, feeding on the fear and uncertainty that had lingered since the battle.

At first, the rumors were dismissed as the idle talk of soldiers who had seen too much and were looking for someone to blame. But as the days passed, the whispers grew louder, more persistent, and more dangerous. They spoke of betrayal, of treachery within the ranks, of a traitor who had been working with the enemy all along.

The whispers were vague at first, lacking specifics or evidence, but they were enough to sow seeds of doubt. Soldiers who had once fought side by side now looked at each other with suspicion, their trust in one another eroded by the constant undercurrent of fear. The alliance, which had been fragile to begin with, began to show signs of strain as old rivalries and grudges resurfaced, fueled by the rumors of betrayal.

Eryndor heard the whispers as well, but they refused to believe them at first. They had fought alongside these soldiers, trusted them with their life, and seen the sacrifices they had made in the battle against the darkness. The idea that one of their own could be working with the enemy seemed unthinkable.

But as the days passed, the whispers became harder to ignore. The tension within the fortress grew, and Eryndor began to notice subtle changes in the behavior of those around them. Conversations stopped when they entered a room, soldiers avoided their gaze, and the air was thick with unspoken accusations.

Eryndor knew that they could not ignore the situation any longer. The rumors, whether true or not, were a threat to the alliance and to the war effort. If the soldiers lost faith in one another, if the alliance fractured, it would weaken their ability to fight the enemy. The prophecy of blood had foretold a great battle, but it had not accounted for the danger that could come from within.

Determined to get to the bottom of the situation, Eryndor called a meeting of the Fallen. They needed to discuss the rumors, to figure out where they had come from and how to put an end to them before they could do any more damage.

The Fallen gathered in a small chamber within the fortress, their expressions grim as they took their seats around the table. The atmosphere was tense, the weight of the situation pressing down on them as they prepared to confront the issue head-on.

Kael was the first to speak, his voice low and serious. "We've all heard the rumors," he said, his eyes scanning the faces of his comrades. "They're spreading like wildfire through the ranks, and they're starting to affect morale. Soldiers are starting to lose trust in one another, and that's a problem we can't afford."

"I've seen it too," Lyra added, her tone sharp with frustration. "Patrols are getting sloppy, and there's been a noticeable increase in tension between the different factions. If this keeps up, it could tear the alliance apart."

Torin nodded in agreement. "The mages are starting to get nervous as well. There have been reports of strange occurrences—magical disturbances that can't be easily explained. Some of them are starting to believe the rumors, and that's making them hesitant to use their magic."

Elara, who had been quiet until now, spoke up, her voice filled with concern. "I've been having visions—dark visions that I can't fully interpret.

But they all point to the same thing: there's a danger within our own ranks, something that threatens to undo everything we've fought for."

Eryndor listened to their concerns, their mind racing as they tried to make sense of the situation. The idea of a traitor in their midst was a chilling one, but they knew that they could not dismiss the possibility. If there was even a chance that someone within the alliance was working with the enemy, they needed to uncover the truth before it was too late.

"We need to find out who's behind these rumors," Eryndor said, their voice firm. "If there's a traitor among us, we need to expose them and put an end to this before it destroys the alliance. But we need to be careful. If we start accusing people without evidence, it could make things even worse."

The Fallen nodded in agreement, their expressions determined. They knew that this would not be an easy task, but they were committed to seeing it through. The stakes were too high to let the situation spiral out of control.

"We'll start by investigating the source of the rumors," Kael suggested. "We need to find out where they started and who's been spreading them. If we can trace them back to their origin, it might give us a clue as to who's behind this."

Lyra leaned forward, her eyes narrowing in thought. "I'll start asking questions, quietly. I know how to get people to talk without raising suspicion. If there's someone spreading these rumors intentionally, I'll find out who it is."

"I'll work with the mages," Torin added. "If there's been any magical tampering, we need to know about it. I'll see if I can identify any traces of dark magic or illusions that might be contributing to the paranoia."

Elara looked at Eryndor, her expression serious. "I'll continue to watch the visions. If I see anything more specific, I'll let you know. But be careful, Eryndor. The enemy is cunning, and they'll use any means necessary to weaken us."

Eryndor nodded, their resolve hardening. "We'll get to the bottom of this. We have to. The fate of the alliance—and the war—depends on it."

The Search for the Traitor

THE DAYS THAT FOLLOWED were tense and filled with uncertainty. The Fallen began their investigation, each working in their own way to uncover the source of the rumors and to determine if there was indeed a traitor within their ranks.

Lyra moved through the fortress like a shadow, listening to the conversations of the soldiers, watching their behavior, and quietly asking questions when the opportunity arose. She was careful not to draw attention to herself, using her skills as an assassin to blend in and gather information without raising suspicion.

She discovered that the rumors had started shortly after the victory at the Dark Fortress, but no one seemed to know exactly where they had originated. Some soldiers claimed to have heard them from a friend, others from a passing conversation, but no one could pinpoint a specific source. It was as if the rumors had appeared out of nowhere, spreading like a poison through the ranks.

Lyra's investigation led her to a group of soldiers who had been stationed near the fortress's eastern wall during the siege. They were a tight-knit group, known for their loyalty to one another, but there was something about their behavior that caught Lyra's attention. They seemed more on edge than the others, their conversations hushed and their eyes wary.

One evening, Lyra approached one of the soldiers, a young man named Jarin, who had been particularly vocal about the rumors. She found him alone in one of the fortress's courtyards, sharpening his sword in the fading light.

"Jarin," she said softly, her voice carrying just enough authority to make him look up. "I've been hearing a lot about these rumors. You've been talking about them quite a bit. Where did you hear them?"

Jarin looked up at her, his eyes narrowing in suspicion. "What's it to you? Everyone's talking about it. You can't tell me you haven't heard."

"I've heard," Lyra replied, her tone calm. "But I'm trying to figure out where they came from. It's important, Jarin. If there's a traitor among us, we need to know."

Jarin hesitated, his gaze shifting to the ground. "I don't know where they started," he muttered. "I just heard it from one of the other guys. We were talking about the siege, about how it went down. And then someone mentioned it—how there was no way the enemy could have known we were coming unless someone told them."

Lyra felt a chill run down her spine. "Who mentioned it?" she pressed.

Jarin shook his head. "I don't remember. It was just talk, you know? People blowing off steam after the battle. But the more I thought about it, the more it made sense. How else could the enemy have been so prepared?"

Lyra frowned. The enemy had indeed been well-prepared for the siege, almost as if they had known in advance that the forces of light were coming. But she couldn't dismiss the possibility that it was simply a matter of the enemy being vigilant and expecting a counterattack.

"Thanks, Jarin," Lyra said, her mind racing as she considered his words. "Be careful what you say. We don't want to cause a panic."

Jarin nodded, his expression uneasy. "Yeah, sure. Just trying to make sense of it all."

As Lyra walked away, she couldn't shake the feeling that there was more to the story. The idea of a traitor within their ranks was terrifying, but it was also possible that the rumors were being spread intentionally—to sow discord and weaken the alliance.

Meanwhile, Torin was working with the mages to investigate the strange magical occurrences that had been reported. He spent hours poring over ancient texts and consulting with the most experienced sorcerers, trying to identify any traces of dark magic that might have been used to influence the soldiers' minds.

He discovered that there had indeed been magical disturbances in the fortress, subtle but powerful. The spells were designed to create an atmosphere of fear and mistrust, amplifying the soldiers' existing doubts and making them more susceptible to suggestion. It was a form of dark magic that was difficult to detect, but Torin was able to trace its origin to a specific area within the fortress.

The source of the magic was a small, hidden chamber deep within the fortress, one that had been overlooked during the initial cleansing after the siege. Torin and a group of mages carefully entered the chamber, their spells at the ready in case of any traps or lingering dark magic.

What they found was a small altar, covered in strange symbols and surrounded by candles that had long since burned out. The air in the chamber was thick with the remnants of dark magic, and Torin could feel the malevolent energy that had been used to cast the spells.

"This is it," Torin said, his voice filled with both triumph and unease. "This is where the spells were cast. Someone has been using this chamber to manipulate the soldiers' minds, to spread fear and distrust."

One of the mages, an elderly man with a long white beard, nodded in agreement. "This is powerful magic—ancient and forbidden. Whoever cast these spells knew what they were doing."

Torin frowned, his thoughts racing. "But who? And why?"

The mage shook his head. "That, we cannot say. But we can cleanse this place, remove the dark magic that lingers here. It will weaken the influence of the spells, but the damage may already be done."

Torin knew that they had to act quickly. If the spells had already taken hold in the minds of the soldiers, it could be difficult to reverse the effects. But at least they had found the source—now they just needed to find out who was behind it.

Elara continued to watch her visions, hoping for a clue that would lead them to the traitor. Her visions were fragmented, showing her glimpses of the future that were difficult to piece together. But one vision stood out to her—a vision of a figure standing in the shadows, their face hidden, but their presence unmistakably malevolent.

In the vision, the figure moved through the fortress, whispering words of deceit and betrayal into the ears of the soldiers. They were a master manipulator, playing on the fears and doubts of those around them, all the while working toward their own dark agenda.

Elara knew that this figure was the key to uncovering the truth, but the vision was unclear, the details obscured. She could not see the figure's face, could not identify them, but she knew that they were close—too close.

Eryndor listened to the reports from the Fallen, their concern growing with each passing day. The evidence was mounting, but they still did not have a clear answer. The idea that someone within the alliance could be working with the enemy was terrifying, but they knew that they had to remain calm, to think strategically.

"We're getting closer," Eryndor said, their voice filled with determination. "But we need more information. We can't act on speculation alone. We need to be sure."

The Fallen nodded in agreement, each of them understanding the gravity of the situation. They knew that time was running out—the longer the traitor remained hidden, the more damage they could do.

But as they continued their investigation, the tension within the fortress grew. The soldiers were on edge, their trust in one another eroded by the constant whispers of betrayal. The alliance was beginning to fracture, old rivalries resurfacing as the different factions began to turn on one another.

Eryndor knew that they had to act quickly, but they also knew that they could not afford to make a mistake. One wrong move could destroy the alliance, and with it, any hope of defeating the darkness.

And then, just when they thought they were out of options, the traitor revealed themselves.

The Betrayer Revealed

IT HAPPENED IN THE dead of night, when most of the fortress was asleep and the guards were at their posts. The air was still, the silence broken only by the distant sound of the wind howling through the mountains.

Eryndor was in their quarters, poring over maps and reports, when they heard a commotion outside. Voices were raised, the sound of boots on stone echoing through the corridors. Something was happening.

They grabbed the Sword of Legends and rushed out of their quarters, following the sound of the commotion. It led them to the central courtyard, where a group of soldiers had gathered, their expressions filled with anger and confusion.

At the center of the courtyard stood Kael the Unbroken, his massive form towering over a smaller figure who was kneeling on the ground, their hands bound behind their back. The figure's head was bowed, their face hidden in the shadows.

"What's going on?" Eryndor demanded as they approached, their eyes narrowing as they took in the scene.

Kael looked up, his expression grim. "We've found the traitor."

Eryndor's heart skipped a beat. "Who?"

Kael stepped aside, revealing the kneeling figure. "It's one of our own."

The figure lifted their head, and Eryndor's breath caught in their throat. It was Jarin—the young soldier Lyra had spoken to just days before. His face was pale, his eyes filled with fear, but there was also something else in his expression—defiance.

"Jarin?" Eryndor said, their voice filled with disbelief. "Why?"

Jarin didn't answer at first, his gaze shifting to the ground. When he finally spoke, his voice was trembling, but there was a hint of anger beneath the fear. "I did what I had to do. You don't understand. None of you do."

"What don't we understand?" Kael demanded, his voice hard.

Jarin looked up, his eyes filled with a mix of desperation and determination. "I didn't have a choice. They came to me—after the battle. They said if I didn't help them, they'd kill my family."

Eryndor felt a surge of anger and pity. "Who came to you? Who forced you to do this?"

Jarin hesitated, his fear palpable. "I don't know who they were. They wore hoods, masks—I couldn't see their faces. But they had power, real power. They showed me what they could do, what they would do if I didn't help them."

"And so you spread the rumors," Lyra said, her voice cold. "You sowed discord among the soldiers, weakened the alliance—all because they threatened you?"

Jarin's expression hardened. "I did what I had to do. You don't know what it's like, to be afraid for the people you love. I didn't want to do it, but what choice did I have?"

Eryndor shook their head, their heart heavy with the weight of the betrayal. "You should have come to us, Jarin. We could have helped you."

Jarin's eyes filled with tears. "You don't understand. They said they had spies everywhere—that if I told anyone, they'd know. I couldn't take that risk."

Kael's expression softened slightly, but his voice remained stern. "And what about the soldiers you betrayed? The ones who trusted you, who fought beside you? What about them?"

Jarin looked away, his voice barely a whisper. "I didn't want to hurt anyone. But I couldn't lose my family. I couldn't."

Eryndor felt a wave of sympathy for Jarin, but they also knew that his actions had put the entire alliance at risk. They couldn't afford to let emotions cloud their judgment.

"We'll deal with this," Eryndor said, their voice firm. "But first, we need to know everything. Who were these people? What did they want?"

Jarin looked up, his expression filled with resignation. "They wanted to weaken the alliance. They knew that if they could make us turn on each other, it would make it easier for them to win. They told me to spread the rumors, to make the soldiers distrust each other. They said it was the only way to protect my family."

Eryndor nodded slowly, their mind racing as they tried to piece together the puzzle. "And where is your family now? Are they safe?"

Jarin's expression crumpled, and he shook his head. "I don't know. They said they'd release them once I'd done what they asked. But I haven't heard anything since."

Eryndor felt a pang of sorrow for the young soldier. He had been manipulated, used as a pawn in a much larger game. But his actions had still caused harm, and they couldn't ignore that.

"Take him to the cells," Eryndor said to Kael. "We'll need to decide what to do with him. But for now, we need to focus on finding these people—whoever they are. They're the real threat."

Kael nodded, and with a heavy heart, he led Jarin away. The soldiers who had gathered in the courtyard began to disperse, their expressions filled with a mix of relief and unease. The traitor had been found, but the damage had already been done.

Eryndor watched them go, their mind heavy with the implications of what had happened. The alliance had been weakened, their trust in one another shaken, but they couldn't afford to let it fall apart. They needed to be strong, united, if they were going to stand a chance against the darkness.

Rebuilding Trust

THE DAYS THAT FOLLOWED were difficult for everyone. The revelation of Jarin's betrayal had sent shockwaves through the fortress, and the soldiers were struggling to come to terms with the fact that one of their own had been working with the enemy. The atmosphere was tense, the camaraderie that had been forged in the heat of battle now strained by the lingering doubt and mistrust.

Eryndor knew that they needed to address the situation head-on if they were going to prevent the alliance from fracturing completely. They called a meeting of the Fallen, determined to find a way to rebuild the trust that had been lost.

"We can't let this destroy us," Eryndor said as they gathered in the same chamber where they had discussed the rumors just days before. "We've come too far, fought too hard, to let one act of betrayal undo everything we've accomplished."

Kael nodded in agreement. "The soldiers are shaken, but they're not broken. They need to see that we're still united, that we're still fighting for the same cause."

"But how do we do that?" Lyra asked, her expression thoughtful. "The damage has been done. The rumors, the distrust—it's all still there, festering beneath the surface. We need to address it, but we need to do it carefully."

Torin spoke up, his voice filled with determination. "We need to remind them why we're here. We need to show them that the fight against the darkness is bigger than any one person, bigger than any one betrayal. If we can do that, we can start to heal the wounds."

Elara, who had been quiet for most of the discussion, finally spoke, her voice calm and measured. "We need to give them something to believe in. The prophecy speaks of a great battle, of a hero who will lead us to victory. But it also speaks of the strength that comes from unity, from standing together in the face of adversity. We need to embody that strength, to show them that we are still united, still determined to see this through."

Eryndor nodded, their resolve hardening. "Then that's what we'll do. We'll address the soldiers, acknowledge what's happened, but also remind them of why we're fighting. We'll show them that we're still united, still committed to the cause. And we'll make it clear that the real enemy is still out there, and that we need to stand together if we're going to defeat them."

The Fallen agreed, and plans were set in motion. The next morning, a gathering was called in the central courtyard, where the soldiers had assembled to hear what Eryndor and the Fallen had to say.

Eryndor stood before the assembled soldiers, their heart heavy with the responsibility that lay on their shoulders. They could see the uncertainty in the soldiers' eyes, the doubt that lingered in the air. But they also saw something else—hope. The soldiers were looking to them for guidance, for reassurance, and Eryndor knew that they couldn't afford to let them down.

"We all know what's happened," Eryndor began, their voice carrying across the courtyard. "A member of our own ranks betrayed us, worked with the enemy to weaken us from within. It's a betrayal that cuts deep, and I know that many of you are struggling to come to terms with it. But we cannot let this act of treachery destroy us. We cannot let it undermine the alliance that we have fought so hard to build."

The soldiers listened in silence, their attention focused on Eryndor's words.

"We are here because we believe in something greater than ourselves," Eryndor continued. "We are here because we believe that the light can triumph over the darkness, that we can protect our homes, our families, and our future. The enemy wants to divide us, to make us turn on each other, because they know that if we stand united, we are unstoppable."

Eryndor looked out over the crowd, their gaze steady. "The prophecy speaks of a great battle, and we are the ones who will fight that battle. But we cannot do it alone. We need each other—every single one of us. We need to trust in one another, to believe in one another, and to fight for one another. Because that is the only way we will win."

The soldiers were silent for a moment, and then one by one, they began to nod in agreement. The tension in the air began to ease, replaced by a renewed sense of determination.

Kael stepped forward, his voice strong and clear. "We are the forces of light, and we will not be defeated. We will stand together, fight together, and win together. Because that is what we must do."

Lyra, Torin, and Elara joined him, each speaking words of encouragement and resolve. The soldiers began to cheer, their voices rising in a chorus of unity and strength.

Eryndor felt a surge of hope as they listened to the cheers of the soldiers. The alliance had been shaken, but it had not been broken. They had faced betrayal, but they had come through it stronger, more united than ever.

The real enemy was still out there, still waiting, but Eryndor knew that they were ready. The prophecy was still unfolding, the battles still to come, but they would face them together, as one.

The light would prevail, because they would make it so.

End of Chapter 7

Chapter 8: The Battle of the Sacred Grove

The Call to the Sacred Grove

The victory at the Dark Fortress and the subsequent revelation of betrayal within their ranks had left the forces of light both stronger and more wary. They had weathered the storm of doubt and discord, but now they faced an even greater challenge. The enemy was regrouping, their dark forces massing for another assault, and this time, they had chosen a battleground of immense significance—the Sacred Grove.

The Sacred Grove was a place of legend, a site of ancient power where the forces of nature and magic converged. It was said to be one of the last remnants of the old world, a place where the very earth thrummed with energy and where the spirits of the ancestors still walked. The grove had been protected for centuries by the druids, a secretive order of guardians who had sworn to preserve its sanctity and to keep its power from falling into the wrong hands.

But now, the darkness had come for the grove. The enemy knew that if they could corrupt the grove's power, they could turn it against the forces of light, using it to fuel their own dark magic and to tip the balance of the war in their favor. The stakes had never been higher, and the forces of light could not afford to let the enemy succeed.

Eryndor stood in the war room of the fortress, the Sword of Legends resting on the table before them. The Fallen were gathered around, their faces grim as they listened to the latest reports from their scouts.

"The enemy is on the move," Kael the Unbroken reported, his voice steady but filled with concern. "They're heading straight for the Sacred Grove. If they reach it, they could use its power to bolster their forces—and we may not be able to stop them."

"The grove is a place of immense power," Torin the Flameborn added, his eyes narrowing in thought. "If the enemy corrupts that power, it could have catastrophic consequences. We have to stop them before they reach it."

Lyra the Shadowblade crossed her arms, her expression tense. "The grove is heavily guarded by the druids, but they won't be able to hold off the enemy on their own. We need to get there first, fortify the grove, and prepare for the battle to come."

Elara the Starseer looked at Eryndor, her voice calm but filled with urgency. "The grove is more than just a place of power—it's a symbol of the old world, of the balance between light and darkness. If we lose it, we lose more than just a battle. We lose a piece of what we're fighting for."

Eryndor nodded, their mind racing as they considered their options. The Sacred Grove was crucial to the balance of power in the world, and they could not allow it to fall into enemy hands. But they also knew that the battle ahead would be unlike any they had faced before. The grove's power was ancient and unpredictable, and they would need to harness it if they were to stand a chance against the enemy.

"We'll move out immediately," Eryndor decided, their voice filled with determination. "We'll take as many forces as we can spare and head for the Sacred Grove. We'll fortify it, protect it, and use its power to turn the tide of battle. This is our chance to strike a decisive blow against the darkness—and we cannot fail."

The Fallen nodded in agreement, their expressions resolute. They knew that the battle ahead would test them in ways they had never been tested before, but they were ready. The Sacred Grove was a place of great power, but it was also a place of great danger. If they could harness that power, they could win the battle. But if they failed, the consequences would be dire.

The Journey to the Grove

THE JOURNEY TO THE Sacred Grove was swift but filled with tension. The forces of light moved with urgency, knowing that time was of the essence. The grove lay deep within the ancient forest of Thaloria, a land of towering trees and thick undergrowth, where the light of the sun barely penetrated the canopy. The forest was a place of mystery and magic, where the line between the physical and the spiritual world was thin.

As they entered the forest, the atmosphere changed. The air grew cooler, the sounds of the world outside fading into a hushed stillness. The trees seemed to watch them as they passed, their branches swaying gently in a breeze that did not reach the ground. It was as if the forest itself was alive, aware of the approaching battle and preparing for what was to come.

Eryndor rode at the head of the column, the Sword of Legends strapped to their side. The sword seemed to pulse with energy as they drew closer to the grove, as if it recognized the power that lay within the heart of the forest. Eryndor could feel the tension in the air, the sense that they were being drawn into something far greater than themselves.

The journey took them deeper and deeper into the forest, the path winding through dense thickets and over ancient roots that had grown thick with age. The light grew dimmer, the shadows longer, until it seemed as if they were moving through a twilight world, where the boundaries between day and night no longer held sway.

Finally, after hours of travel, they reached the edge of the Sacred Grove. The grove was a circular clearing, surrounded by towering trees that seemed to form a natural barrier against the outside world. At the center of the grove stood a massive stone altar, covered in intricate carvings that glowed faintly in the dim light. The ground beneath their feet was soft with moss, and the air was filled with the scent of earth and growing things.

The druids were already there, their presence almost ethereal as they moved through the grove, tending to the ancient trees and preparing for the battle to come. They were a secretive order, their faces hidden beneath hoods and their voices low as they chanted ancient prayers to the spirits of the forest.

Eryndor dismounted and approached the druids, the Fallen close behind. The leader of the druids, a tall figure with a staff made of twisted wood, stepped forward to greet them.

"Welcome to the Sacred Grove," the druid leader said, their voice calm but filled with a deep, resonant power. "We have been expecting you."

Eryndor nodded in greeting. "We've come to protect the grove—and to use its power to fight the darkness."

The druid leader inclined their head. "The grove is a place of great power, but it is also a place of great danger. The spirits of the forest are ancient and powerful, but they do not take sides in the wars of men. If you wish to harness their power, you must prove yourselves worthy."

"We understand the risks," Eryndor replied. "But we have no choice. The enemy is coming, and if they take the grove, they will use its power to destroy everything we've fought for."

The druid leader studied Eryndor for a moment, their eyes hidden beneath their hood. "Very well. We will assist you in fortifying the grove and preparing for the battle. But remember this: the grove's power is not to be taken lightly. If you lose control of it, it could destroy you as easily as it destroys your enemies."

Eryndor nodded, their resolve firm. "We'll do whatever it takes."

The druids moved to assist the forces of light in preparing the grove for the battle. The trees at the edge of the grove were fortified with magical barriers, their roots and branches woven together to form a natural wall that would protect the clearing from the enemy's advance. The altar at the center of the grove was surrounded by a circle of stones, each inscribed with ancient runes that pulsed with energy.

As the preparations continued, Eryndor and the Fallen took a moment to survey the grove. The air was thick with magic, the very ground beneath their feet thrumming with energy. It was a place of immense power, but it was also a place of balance, where light and darkness coexisted in a delicate harmony.

"This place is incredible," Torin said, his voice filled with awe. "The power here—it's like nothing I've ever felt before."

"It's ancient," Elara added, her voice soft. "Older than anything we've encountered. The spirits here are strong—they're watching us, waiting to see what we'll do."

Lyra nodded, her expression thoughtful. "We need to be careful. The enemy will try to corrupt this power, to turn it against us. We can't let that happen."

Kael gripped his warhammer tightly, his resolve clear. "We'll hold the line. We won't let them take this place."

Eryndor looked at their friends, their comrades, and felt a surge of determination. The Sacred Grove was a place of great power, but it was also a place of great responsibility. They had come to protect it, to harness its power for the fight against the darkness, and they would not fail.

The sun began to set, casting long shadows across the grove. The air grew colder, the sky darkening as night fell over the forest. The forces of light took their positions, readying themselves for the battle to come. The druids continued their chants, their voices rising and falling in a rhythmic cadence that seemed to resonate with the very earth itself.

And then, as the last light of day faded from the sky, the enemy arrived.

The Clash of Forces

THE FIRST SIGN OF THE enemy's approach was a low rumble, like distant thunder, that echoed through the forest. The ground beneath their feet trembled, the trees swaying as if in response to some unseen force. The druids ceased their chanting, their heads turning toward the edge of the grove, where the darkness had begun to gather.

The forces of light stood ready, their weapons drawn and their hearts steeled for the fight. The air was thick with tension, the silence before the storm, as they waited for the enemy to reveal themselves.

And then, with a deafening roar, the darkness surged forward.

The enemy's forces were vast and terrifying—an army of shadowy creatures, twisted by dark magic, their forms barely visible in the dim light. They moved with unnatural speed, their eyes glowing with malevolent intent, and at their head were the dark sorcerers, their hands crackling with forbidden power.

The battle began with a clash of steel and magic, the forces of light meeting the enemy head-on. Kael led the charge, his warhammer smashing through the ranks of the shadowy creatures with brutal force. He fought with the strength of a man who had lost everything and had nothing left to lose, his presence a rallying point for the soldiers who fought beside him.

Lyra moved through the shadows, her twin daggers flashing in the dim light. She struck with deadly precision, her movements fluid and graceful as she danced through the enemy's ranks. She was a whirlwind of death, her every strike a testament to her skill as an assassin.

Torin stood at the rear, his hands glowing with the power of fire. He unleashed waves of flame upon the enemy, his magic searing through the darkness and weakening the enemy's advance. The flames illuminated the grove, casting eerie shadows that danced across the trees and the altar at its center.

Elara used her gift of foresight to guide the forces of light, her visions allowing her to anticipate the enemy's movements and to warn her allies of impending danger. She was a calming presence amidst the chaos of battle, her wisdom and insight helping the soldiers to stay focused and to press forward despite the odds.

Eryndor fought at the forefront, the Sword of Legends blazing with a light that cut through the darkness. The sword's power was immense, its light searing through the enemy's defenses and weakening their hold on the grove. But even with the sword's power, Eryndor knew that they could not win the battle alone. They needed to harness the power of the grove, to use it to tip the balance in their favor.

As the battle raged on, the enemy's forces began to push deeper into the grove. The dark sorcerers chanted incantations, their magic warping the very fabric of the grove's power, twisting it to their will. The trees at the edge of the grove began to wither, their leaves turning black as the corruption spread.

Eryndor knew that they had to act quickly. The grove's power was ancient and unpredictable, but it was also their only hope. If they could harness it, they could turn the tide of the battle and drive the enemy back.

With a cry of determination, Eryndor raised the Sword of Legends high and called upon the power of the grove. The sword pulsed with energy, its light growing brighter as it resonated with the magic of the grove. The ground beneath their feet began to tremble, the air filled with a low hum as the grove's power awakened.

The druids joined in, their chants rising in pitch as they called upon the spirits of the forest to aid in the battle. The stones around the altar glowed brighter, the runes etched upon them pulsing with energy. The very earth seemed to come alive, the trees and plants responding to the call of the druids.

The enemy hesitated, their advance faltering as the power of the grove surged through the battlefield. The shadowy creatures recoiled, their forms flickering as if struggling to maintain their shape. The dark sorcerers redoubled their efforts, their voices rising in a desperate attempt to maintain control of the corrupted magic.

But the grove's power was stronger, older, and more resilient than they had anticipated. The spirits of the forest answered the call, their presence filling the grove with a palpable energy that pushed back the darkness. The corrupted trees at the edge of the grove began to heal, their leaves returning to their natural green as the corruption was purged.

Eryndor felt the power of the grove flow through them, the Sword of Legends acting as a conduit for the ancient magic. They could feel the spirits of the forest around them, guiding their hand as they struck down the enemy with renewed strength. The light of the sword grew brighter, its power overwhelming the darkness that sought to consume the grove.

The forces of light rallied, their spirits lifted by the surge of energy. Kael led the soldiers in a renewed assault, his warhammer striking with the force of a battering ram. Lyra moved through the shadows with even greater speed, her daggers finding their mark with unerring precision. Torin's flames burned hotter, the fire magic bolstered by the power of the grove. Elara's visions became clearer, her guidance more precise as she directed the forces of light with unwavering confidence.

The enemy began to falter, their forces pushed back by the combined strength of the grove and the forces of light. The dark sorcerers fought desperately to maintain their hold on the corrupted magic, but it was a losing battle. The spirits of the forest were too strong, their connection to the grove too deep to be severed.

With one final, desperate effort, the dark sorcerers unleashed a wave of dark magic, their voices raised in a cacophony of incantations. The magic surged through the grove, a black tide that sought to drown the light in darkness.

But Eryndor was ready. They raised the Sword of Legends high, calling upon the full power of the grove. The sword blazed with a light that outshone the sun, a pure, brilliant light that cut through the darkness like a beacon of hope.

The dark magic faltered, unable to withstand the combined power of the sword and the grove. The tide of darkness was pushed back, the shadowy creatures disintegrating into nothingness as the light overwhelmed them. The dark sorcerers screamed in defiance, their forms consumed by the very magic they had sought to control.

The grove erupted in a burst of light, the energy of the spirits washing over the battlefield and purging the last remnants of the enemy's corruption. The ground trembled, the air filled with a roar that seemed to come from the very heart of the earth.

And then, as suddenly as it had begun, the battle was over.

The Aftermath

THE SACRED GROVE WAS silent, the only sound the soft rustle of leaves in the gentle breeze. The air was filled with the scent of earth and growing things, the power of the grove thrumming gently beneath the surface.

The forces of light stood victorious, their weapons lowered as they surveyed the battlefield. The enemy was gone, their forces destroyed by the combined power of the grove and the Sword of Legends. The grove had been saved, its ancient magic preserved and its spirits at peace.

Eryndor stood at the center of the grove, the Sword of Legends still glowing faintly in their hand. They could feel the energy of the grove around them, the spirits of the forest watching over them with a sense of quiet approval. The battle had been fierce, but they had prevailed.

The druids approached, their hoods pulled back to reveal their faces. The druid leader stepped forward, their expression filled with respect.

"You have proven yourselves worthy," the druid leader said, their voice resonant with the power of the grove. "The spirits of the forest have accepted you, and they will aid you in the battles to come."

Eryndor nodded, their heart filled with gratitude. "Thank you. We couldn't have done it without your help."

"The grove is a place of balance," the druid leader continued. "A place where light and darkness coexist. You have restored that balance, and in doing so, you have strengthened the light. But remember this: the battle is not yet over. The darkness still lurks in the shadows, waiting for its chance to strike."

"We know," Eryndor replied, their voice firm. "But we'll be ready. The enemy won't take us by surprise again."

The druid leader inclined their head. "Then go with the blessings of the grove. The spirits will watch over you, and their power will be with you in the battles to come."

As the druids returned to their duties, the Fallen gathered around Eryndor. Their faces were tired, but their spirits were high. They had faced the darkness in one of its most powerful forms, and they had emerged victorious.

"That was something else," Torin said, his voice filled with awe. "I've never felt power like that before."

"The grove is ancient," Elara added, her voice soft. "Older than anything we've encountered. But it's also a place of hope, a reminder of what we're fighting for."

Kael nodded, his expression serious. "We've dealt a heavy blow to the enemy today. But Elara's right—the war isn't over yet. We need to stay vigilant."

Lyra looked at Eryndor, her eyes filled with respect. "You did well, Eryndor. You harnessed the power of the grove and used it to turn the tide of battle. The enemy won't forget that."

Eryndor felt a sense of pride, but also a deep responsibility. The Sacred Grove had given them the strength they needed to win the battle, but it had also shown them the true nature of the war they were fighting. This was more than just a battle between armies—it was a battle for the very soul of the world, a battle to preserve the balance between light and darkness.

As they prepared to leave the grove, Eryndor took one last look at the ancient trees, the stone altar, and the runes that glowed faintly in the dim light. The grove was a place of great power, but it was also a place of peace, a place where the forces of nature and magic coexisted in harmony.

The battle had been won, but the war was far from over. The prophecy of blood was still unfolding, the darkness still waiting in the shadows. But Eryndor knew that they were ready. They had faced the enemy in one of its most powerful forms and had emerged victorious.

The Sacred Grove had given them the strength they needed, and they would carry that strength with them in the battles to come.

As they left the grove and made their way back through the ancient forest, the spirits of the forest watched over them, their presence a comforting reminder that they were not alone in the fight against the darkness.

The light had triumphed in the Battle of the Sacred Grove, but the true test was yet to come.

END OF CHAPTER 8

Chapter 9: The Fall of the Great City

The Threat Looms

The Great City of Eldoria, often called the Jewel of the East, had long been a symbol of prosperity, strength, and resilience. Its towering walls, which had withstood countless sieges, protected a bustling metropolis that was the heart of trade, culture, and knowledge in the eastern lands. The city was a beacon of hope, a place where the light of civilization shone brightest even as the darkness gathered at the edges of the world.

But that light was now in peril. The enemy, emboldened by their previous skirmishes and driven by a malevolent will, had set their sights on Eldoria. Rumors of the approaching army had spread through the allied forces like wildfire, bringing with them a sense of dread that was difficult to dispel. The enemy's strategy was clear: by capturing Eldoria, they would strike a devastating blow to the morale of the allied forces and secure a strategic foothold that could turn the tide of the war in their favor.

Eryndor, along with the Fallen and the commanders of the allied forces, gathered in the war room of the Sacred Grove to discuss their next move. The mood was tense, the air heavy with the weight of the decisions that needed to be made. The map of Eldoria and its surrounding territories lay spread out on the table before them, marked with the latest intelligence reports on enemy movements.

"We can't let Eldoria fall," Kael the Unbroken said, his voice filled with determination. "The city is too important—both strategically and symbolically. If the enemy takes it, we'll lose more than just a stronghold. We'll lose the faith of the people."

"The city is well-fortified," Lyra the Shadowblade added, her tone measured. "But it's also vulnerable. The enemy has been targeting our supply lines, and the city's defenses are stretched thin. They've been preparing for this attack for some time."

Torin the Flameborn leaned over the map, his brow furrowed in thought. "We need to reinforce the city as quickly as possible. If we can hold the walls, we might be able to buy enough time to regroup and launch a counteroffensive."

Elara the Starseer, her eyes distant as she gazed into the future, spoke softly but with a sense of urgency. "The enemy's assault will be relentless. I've seen visions of fire and blood, of walls crumbling and people fleeing in terror. But I've also seen glimpses of hope—of survivors finding the strength to resist, even in the face of overwhelming odds."

Eryndor listened to their comrades, their mind racing as they considered the situation. Eldoria was indeed a critical stronghold, and its loss would be a severe blow to the allied forces. But they also knew that the enemy was cunning, and that their attack on Eldoria was part of a larger strategy to weaken the alliance from within.

"We need to send reinforcements to Eldoria," Eryndor decided, their voice steady. "But we also need to prepare for the possibility that the city may fall. We can't afford to put all our resources into defending it, or we'll leave ourselves vulnerable elsewhere. We need to be strategic—send enough forces to bolster the city's defenses, but keep enough in reserve to respond to other threats."

The Fallen nodded in agreement, understanding the difficult balance that needed to be struck. The defense of Eldoria was crucial, but it was not the only front in the war. The enemy was relentless, and they would seize any opportunity to exploit weaknesses in the allied forces.

"Who will lead the defense of Eldoria?" Kael asked, his gaze turning to Eryndor.

Eryndor considered the question carefully. The defense of the city required a leader who was not only skilled in battle but also capable of inspiring the troops and the city's inhabitants to stand firm in the face of overwhelming odds.

"I will lead the defense," Eryndor finally said, their decision firm. "The Sword of Legends will be needed to rally the defenders and to harness whatever power we can from the city's ancient defenses. The rest of you will stay here and coordinate our response to any other threats that arise."

The decision was met with nods of approval from the Fallen. They knew that Eryndor's presence in Eldoria would be a powerful symbol of resistance, and that their leadership could make the difference between victory and defeat.

"We'll do everything we can to support you from here," Lyra said, her voice filled with determination. "And if the city falls, we'll be ready to regroup and continue the fight."

Eryndor nodded, their resolve unshaken. "Then it's settled. We leave for Eldoria at once."

The Defense of Eldoria

THE JOURNEY TO ELDORIA was swift and filled with a sense of urgency. The allied forces, bolstered by reinforcements from neighboring territories, moved with purpose as they approached the Great City. As they neared the city, the signs of the enemy's approach became evident—burned-out villages, abandoned farms, and the distant sound of marching feet that sent chills down the spine.

When they finally reached Eldoria, the city was already preparing for the impending siege. The streets were filled with soldiers, their faces grim as they reinforced the walls and prepared their weapons. Civilians were being evacuated to the city's inner sanctum, where they would be safe from the initial assault. The mood was one of determination mixed with fear, the knowledge that the enemy was at their gates weighing heavily on the hearts of the defenders.

Eryndor took command of the city's defenses, meeting with the local commanders and the city's ruling council to discuss their strategy. The walls of Eldoria were strong, but the enemy's numbers were vast, and the city's defenders were outnumbered. They would need to rely on more than just physical defenses to hold the city—they would need to harness the ancient magic that had protected Eldoria for centuries.

The city's ruling council, made up of scholars, mages, and seasoned warriors, had long guarded the secrets of Eldoria's defenses. The city was built on a nexus of ley lines, channels of magical energy that crisscrossed the land. These ley lines converged beneath the city's central keep, where a powerful artifact known as the Heartstone was housed. The Heartstone was the source of the city's protective wards, a crystal of immense power that had been passed down through generations.

Eryndor, along with the city's head mage, a wise and experienced sorcerer named Master Arlen, descended into the depths of the keep to examine the Heartstone. The chamber that housed the artifact was a place of ancient power, its walls inscribed with runes that glowed faintly in the dim light. The Heartstone itself was a large, multifaceted crystal that pulsed with a steady, rhythmic light, its power palpable in the air.

"This is the Heartstone," Master Arlen said, his voice reverent. "It has protected Eldoria for centuries, but its power is not infinite. The enemy will try to breach the wards it maintains, and if they succeed, the city will be vulnerable."

Eryndor approached the Heartstone, feeling the power emanating from it. The Sword of Legends, which they carried with them, seemed to resonate with the crystal, the two artifacts sharing a deep connection through the ley lines.

"Can we strengthen the wards?" Eryndor asked, their voice filled with determination.

Master Arlen nodded. "Yes, but it will require a great deal of energy. The Heartstone can draw upon the ley lines, but we must channel that energy carefully. If we push it too far, we risk overloading the wards, which could cause them to fail entirely."

Eryndor considered the situation carefully. They needed to strengthen the city's defenses, but they also needed to conserve the Heartstone's power for the inevitable breach. The enemy would not give up easily, and they needed to be prepared for a prolonged siege.

"Strengthen the wards as much as you can," Eryndor instructed. "But keep enough power in reserve to repair any breaches. We'll need every advantage we can get."

Master Arlen nodded in agreement and began the process of channeling the ley lines' energy into the Heartstone. The crystal glowed brighter, the runes on the walls of the chamber flaring with light as the wards around the city were reinforced.

With the city's defenses bolstered, Eryndor returned to the walls, where the soldiers were making their final preparations for the siege. The enemy was drawing closer, their vanguard already visible on the horizon. The air was thick with tension, the knowledge that the battle was imminent weighing heavily on the hearts of the defenders.

As the sun began to set, casting a blood-red glow across the sky, the enemy's forces finally arrived. They were a terrifying sight—an army of darkness that stretched as far as the eye could see, their ranks filled with twisted creatures, undead soldiers, and dark sorcerers. The ground beneath them seemed to wither and die as they marched, the very air around them thick with the stench of death and decay.

Eryndor stood at the forefront of the city's defenses, the Sword of Legends glowing with a fierce light. The soldiers around them looked to their leader for guidance, their resolve strengthened by Eryndor's presence. The fate of Eldoria rested on their shoulders, and they knew that they could not fail.

The enemy's assault began with a thunderous roar, a wave of dark magic crashing against the city's wards. The ground shook, the walls trembling under the force of the attack, but the wards held firm, their power bolstered by the Heartstone's energy. The enemy's forces surged forward, crashing against the walls like a tide of darkness, but the defenders stood strong, repelling the assault with arrows, spells, and steel.

The battle raged throughout the night, the sounds of combat echoing through the city as the defenders fought with everything they had. The enemy's forces were relentless, their dark sorcerers casting spells of destruction that threatened to breach the city's wards. But the defenders held the line, their determination unyielding as they fought to protect their home.

Eryndor moved through the battle with the grace of a seasoned warrior, the Sword of Legends cutting through the enemy with a brilliance that lit up the night. They could feel the power of the Heartstone coursing through the city's wards, the ley lines beneath their feet thrumming with energy as they channeled the ancient magic into their strikes.

Kael led the soldiers on the walls, his warhammer smashing through the ranks of the enemy with brutal force. He fought with the strength of a man who had nothing left to lose, his presence a rallying point for the defenders. Lyra moved through the shadows, her twin daggers striking down the dark sorcerers who sought to weaken the city's wards. Torin unleashed waves of fire, his magic searing through the darkness and forcing the enemy to retreat. Elara's visions guided the defenders, allowing them to anticipate the enemy's movements and to counter their attacks with precision.

But as the night wore on, the enemy's assault grew more intense. The dark sorcerers began to focus their attacks on the Heartstone itself, their spells designed to disrupt the ley lines and weaken the city's wards. The ground beneath the city began to tremble, the wards flickering as the Heartstone struggled to maintain its power.

Eryndor could feel the strain on the city's defenses, the pressure mounting as the enemy's forces continued their relentless assault. The Heartstone was powerful, but it was not invincible. They needed to find a way to turn the tide of the battle, or the city would fall.

The Fall of Eldoria

AS DAWN APPROACHED, the enemy launched a final, all-out assault on the city. The dark sorcerers gathered their power, casting a massive spell that struck the Heartstone with the force of a hammer blow. The ground shook violently, the wards around the city flaring brightly before shattering like glass.

The walls of Eldoria, once impenetrable, began to crumble. The enemy's forces surged forward, pouring through the breaches in the city's defenses. The defenders fought valiantly, but they were overwhelmed by the sheer numbers of the enemy. The streets of Eldoria, once filled with life and laughter, became a battleground, the air filled with the sounds of combat and the cries of the wounded.

Eryndor fought desperately to rally the defenders, the Sword of Legends blazing with light as they cut through the enemy's ranks. But even they could see that the battle was lost. The city was falling, and there was nothing they could do to stop it.

"Fall back!" Eryndor shouted, their voice carrying over the chaos. "Retreat to the inner sanctum! We need to protect the civilians!"

The defenders began to pull back, fighting a desperate rearguard action as they retreated toward the central keep. The enemy pressed their advantage, their forces flooding into the city and overwhelming the defenders with sheer numbers.

Kael, Lyra, Torin, and Elara fought alongside Eryndor, their faces grim as they realized the gravity of the situation. They had given everything they had, but it had not been enough. The enemy's power was too great, their numbers too overwhelming.

As they reached the inner sanctum, the doors of the keep were thrown open, and the civilians who had taken refuge within were hurriedly evacuated through a series of hidden tunnels that led out of the city. The ruling council, their faces filled with sorrow, handed Eryndor a small, ornate box containing the Heartstone, now dim and drained of its power.

"Take it," the head of the council said, his voice heavy with emotion. "It is all that remains of Eldoria's power. Protect it, and ensure that its light is not extinguished."

Eryndor took the box, their heart heavy with the weight of their failure. They had come to protect the city, but they had not been able to save it. The fall of Eldoria would be a devastating blow to the allied forces, both strategically and symbolically.

But there was no time for regret. The enemy was closing in, and they needed to ensure the safety of the civilians and the Heartstone. The survivors of the city's fall made their way through the tunnels, their footsteps echoing through the darkness as they fled the city that had been their home.

As they emerged from the tunnels, they could see the Great City of Eldoria burning in the distance, its once-proud walls now crumbling and engulfed in flames. The enemy's banners flew over the city, a stark reminder of the price that had been paid.

Eryndor stood with the Fallen and the survivors on a hill overlooking the city, their hearts heavy with the loss. The fall of Eldoria was a devastating blow, one that would be felt throughout the allied forces. But even in the face of such despair, there was a glimmer of hope—a determination to continue the fight, to honor the sacrifices that had been made, and to ensure that the enemy's victory was not complete.

The Aftermath

THE FALL OF ELDORIA sent shockwaves through the allied forces. The news of the city's capture spread quickly, bringing with it a sense of despair and uncertainty. The Great City had been a symbol of hope, and its loss was a devastating blow to the morale of the soldiers and civilians alike.

But even in the face of such a crushing defeat, the survivors of Eldoria showed remarkable resilience. The civilians who had fled the city began to regroup in nearby villages and strongholds, determined to continue the fight. The ruling council, now displaced and without a city to govern, pledged their support to the allied forces, vowing to use their knowledge and resources to aid in the war effort.

Eryndor and the Fallen returned to the Sacred Grove, their hearts heavy with the weight of their failure. But they knew that the war was far from over, and that they could not afford to dwell on the past. The enemy's victory in Eldoria was a setback, but it was not the end. The allied forces would regroup, recalibrate their strategy, and continue the fight.

The Heartstone, though drained of its power, was still a symbol of hope. Master Arlen and the mages of the Sacred Grove began the delicate process of recharging the artifact, drawing upon the ley lines to restore its energy. It would take time, but they were determined to ensure that the Heartstone would once again be a source of light and power in the battle against the darkness.

As the allied forces gathered in the Sacred Grove, Eryndor addressed the survivors and the commanders. Their voice was steady, their resolve unshaken, as they spoke of the challenges that lay ahead.

"Eldoria has fallen," Eryndor said, their voice carrying over the assembled crowd. "But we have not. The enemy may have taken the city, but they have not taken our will to fight. We will regroup, we will rebuild, and we will continue the fight. The fall of Eldoria is a reminder of the stakes in this war, but it is also a reminder of our strength. We have faced adversity before, and we have overcome it. We will do so again."

The crowd listened in silence, their expressions a mix of sorrow and determination. They had lost much, but they had not lost everything. The war was far from over, and they were still in the fight.

"We will honor the sacrifices that were made," Eryndor continued. "We will honor the memory of those who gave their lives to protect Eldoria. And we will ensure that their sacrifice was not in vain. The enemy may have won a battle, but they have not won the war. We will continue to fight, to resist, and to protect what we hold dear. The light will prevail—because we will make it so."

As Eryndor finished speaking, the crowd erupted in cheers, their spirits lifted by the words of their leader. The fall of Eldoria was a devastating blow, but it had not broken them. They were still standing, still fighting, and still determined to see the war through to its end.

The strategic recalibrations began immediately. The allied forces restructured their defenses, fortifying key strongholds and shoring up supply lines. They began to gather intelligence on the enemy's movements, preparing for the next phase of the war. The loss of Eldoria had forced them to adapt, to rethink their strategy, but it had also brought them closer together, united by the shared determination to protect their world from the darkness.

The Fallen played a crucial role in these efforts, their experience and leadership invaluable as the allied forces prepared for the battles to come. Kael took charge of training the soldiers, ensuring that they were ready for the next encounter with the enemy. Lyra worked with the scouts and spies, gathering intelligence on the enemy's plans. Torin continued to work with the mages, refining their magical defenses and preparing for the possibility of another siege. Elara used her visions to guide the strategic planning, her foresight helping to anticipate the enemy's next moves.

Eryndor, meanwhile, focused on restoring the Heartstone and preparing for the next confrontation with the enemy. They knew that the fall of Eldoria was not the end—it was merely the beginning of a new chapter in the war. The enemy had gained a foothold, but the allied forces were far from defeated. The fight would continue, and they would do whatever it took to protect their world from the darkness.

The fall of the Great City was a harsh reminder of the

stakes in the war, but it was also a testament to the resilience of the allied forces. They had faced a devastating loss, but they had not given up. They had regrouped, recalibrated, and prepared to continue the fight.

The war was far from over, but the light had not been extinguished. It still burned brightly in the hearts of those who fought for a better future.

And as long as that light remained, there was hope.

END OF CHAPTER 9

Chapter 10: The Spirit of the Ancestors

The Weight of the Prophecy

The fall of the Great City had left Eryndor and the allied forces reeling. Though they had regrouped and recalibrated their strategy, the loss weighed heavily on them, especially on Eryndor. The burden of leadership, the constant threat of the enemy, and the fear of further losses had begun to take their toll. The prophecy that had driven them this far was both a source of hope and a source of fear—it foretold victory, but at what cost? The uncertainty of their role in this grand design gnawed at Eryndor, who felt the crushing weight of expectations and the fear of failure.

In the days following the fall of Eldoria, Eryndor found themselves restless, unable to shake the feeling that they were missing something crucial. The prophecy had guided their actions, but it had also left many questions unanswered. What did it truly mean to be the Chosen One? What sacrifices would they be asked to make? And what would be the final outcome of this war?

As these questions swirled in their mind, Eryndor became increasingly aware of a sense of emptiness—a void where certainty should have been. They realized that they needed guidance, wisdom from those who had faced similar trials, who had seen the ebb and flow of battles, and who could offer insight into the prophecy that weighed so heavily on their shoulders.

It was then that Eryndor decided to seek the guidance of the spirits of their ancestors.

The idea came to them during a rare moment of calm, as they stood alone on a hill overlooking the Sacred Grove. The night was clear, the sky filled with stars that twinkled like distant flames in the darkness. The air was cool, and the sounds of the night creatures filled the stillness with a sense of life and continuity, a reminder that the world carried on even in the midst of war.

Eryndor had heard tales of the ancestors—mighty warriors, wise leaders, and powerful sorcerers who had guided their people through times of great peril. It was said that these spirits, though long departed from the mortal realm, still watched over their descendants, offering guidance in times of need. The Sacred Grove, with its ancient power and connection to the spiritual world, seemed the perfect place to seek them out.

Determined to find the answers they sought, Eryndor descended from the hill and made their way to the heart of the Sacred Grove, where the ley lines converged and where the barrier between the physical and spiritual worlds was said to be thinnest.

The Journey to the Spirit World

THE JOURNEY TO THE heart of the Sacred Grove was short but filled with a sense of anticipation. The trees that surrounded the grove seemed to lean in closer as Eryndor passed, their branches whispering secrets of the old world, secrets that only those attuned to the magic of the land could hear. The ground beneath their feet was soft with moss, the air heavy with the scent of earth and ancient wood.

As Eryndor approached the central clearing, they could feel the power of the ley lines thrumming beneath the surface, a steady pulse of energy that resonated with the Sword of Legends, which they carried with them. The sword had become an extension of themselves, its power intertwined with their own destiny, and it seemed to hum in response to the magic that filled the grove.

In the center of the clearing stood a large stone altar, covered in moss and inscribed with runes that glowed faintly in the moonlight. The altar was ancient, older than the city of Eldoria, older even than the Sacred Grove itself. It had been placed there by the first druids, who had recognized the power of the ley lines and had built the altar as a conduit to the spiritual world.

Eryndor approached the altar, their heart pounding with a mix of excitement and trepidation. They knew that what they were about to attempt was dangerous—calling upon the spirits of the ancestors was not something to be taken lightly. The spirits were powerful, and they did not suffer fools. But

Eryndor was determined. They needed answers, and they were willing to take the risk to find them.

Kneeling before the altar, Eryndor placed the Sword of Legends on the stone surface, its blade glowing faintly in the moonlight. They closed their eyes and began to focus, reaching out with their mind to the ley lines that pulsed beneath the earth. They could feel the energy coursing through the ground, flowing into the altar, and from there into the sword, which acted as a conduit for their will.

Eryndor began to chant, their voice low and steady as they recited the ancient words that had been passed down through generations. The language was old, older than any they had ever spoken, but the words came naturally to them, as if they had been etched into their very soul.

As they chanted, the runes on the altar began to glow brighter, the energy of the ley lines flowing into the stone and resonating with the sword. The air around them grew thick with magic, the temperature dropping as the boundary between the physical and spiritual worlds began to blur.

Eryndor could feel the presence of the spirits drawing closer, their energy swirling around them like a whirlwind. They continued to chant, their voice growing louder as they called out to the ancestors, seeking their guidance, their wisdom, and their strength.

And then, with a sudden rush of energy, the spirits answered.

The Council of the Ancestors

THE WORLD AROUND ERYNDOR seemed to shift, the physical world fading away as they were drawn into the spirit realm. The grove, the altar, even the sword seemed to dissolve into mist, leaving Eryndor standing in a vast, empty space filled with a soft, otherworldly light. The air was still, the silence profound, as if the very world was holding its breath.

Eryndor stood alone in the center of the spirit realm, the weight of the prophecy still heavy on their shoulders. But now, they were no longer in the physical world. They had crossed the threshold, entered a place where time and space held little meaning, a place where the spirits of the ancestors resided.

As they stood there, the light around them began to shift and coalesce, forming shapes that gradually took on more defined forms. Eryndor watched in awe as the spirits of their ancestors appeared before them—mighty warriors clad in armor, wise sorcerers with staffs of power, and noble leaders whose presence commanded respect and reverence.

The spirits formed a circle around Eryndor, their faces calm and serene, their eyes filled with a wisdom that came from centuries of experience. They were the guardians of the past, the keepers of the old ways, and the protectors of the future. Each of them had faced their own trials, fought their own battles, and now, they stood before Eryndor, ready to offer their guidance.

One of the spirits, a tall warrior with a scarred face and a sword that seemed to shimmer with the light of a thousand stars, stepped forward. His presence was commanding, his gaze piercing as he looked down at Eryndor.

"Chosen One," the warrior spirit said, his voice deep and resonant, echoing through the spirit realm. "You have called upon us, the spirits of your ancestors. We have watched over you, seen the trials you have faced, and now we stand before you. What is it you seek?"

Eryndor took a deep breath, their heart pounding as they faced the spirits of their ancestors. They could feel the weight of their gaze, the expectation that they would prove themselves worthy of the title of Chosen One.

"I seek guidance," Eryndor replied, their voice steady despite the nerves that churned within them. "The prophecy has brought me this far, but there is so much I do not understand. I do not know what my true role is, what sacrifices I must make, or what the final outcome of this war will be. I need to know how to fulfill my destiny, how to ensure that the light prevails."

The warrior spirit nodded, his expression thoughtful. "The prophecy is a powerful force, but it is not always clear. It speaks in riddles, in symbols, and it can be difficult to discern its true meaning. But you are not alone in this, Chosen One. We, your ancestors, have faced similar trials, and we can offer you the wisdom you seek."

Another spirit stepped forward, this one an elderly sorcerer with a long white beard and eyes that seemed to glow with inner light. He carried a staff made of twisted wood, and his presence exuded a sense of calm and serenity.

"The prophecy speaks of a great battle," the sorcerer spirit said, his voice soft but filled with authority. "But it also speaks of balance, of the need to maintain harmony between the forces of light and darkness. You, Chosen One, are the key to this balance. Your role is not just to fight, but to understand the forces at play, to bring them into alignment so that the world can be saved."

Eryndor listened intently, their mind racing as they tried to grasp the meaning of the sorcerer's words. Balance? Alignment? They had always thought their role was to lead the forces of light to victory, to defeat the darkness once and for all. But now, the spirits were suggesting that there was more to the prophecy than they had realized.

A third spirit, a noble leader with a crown of gold and a robe of deep crimson, stepped forward. Her eyes were wise and compassionate, her presence radiating a sense of authority that was tempered by empathy.

"The path of the Chosen One is not an easy one," the leader spirit

said, her voice filled with a gentle strength. "You will be asked to make sacrifices, to endure hardships that few can imagine. But you must also remember that you are not alone. The forces of light are with you, the people you fight for are with you, and we, your ancestors, are with you. Do not carry this burden alone, Eryndor. Share it with those who stand by your side, and you will find the strength to continue."

Eryndor felt a wave of emotion wash over them as they listened to the spirits. The wisdom they offered was profound, but it also carried a heavy truth. The prophecy was not just about fighting and winning—it was about understanding, about bringing balance to a world that was teetering on the edge of chaos. And to do that, Eryndor would need to rely on the strength of those around them, to trust in their allies, and to embrace the role they had been given, even if it meant making difficult choices.

The warrior spirit stepped forward once more, his gaze steady as he looked into Eryndor's eyes. "There is one more thing you must understand, Chosen One. The prophecy is not set in stone. It is a guide, a path that you must walk, but the choices you make along the way will shape its outcome. You have the power to influence the course of events, to tip the balance in favor of the light. But you must be wise, be strong, and be true to yourself."

Eryndor felt a sense of clarity begin to form in their mind, the pieces of the puzzle slowly falling into place. The prophecy was not a rigid decree—it was a living, breathing force that they could shape through their actions, their decisions. Their role was not just to fight, but to guide, to lead, and to bring about the balance that the world so desperately needed.

"I understand," Eryndor said, their voice filled with newfound determination. "I will do what is necessary to fulfill the prophecy, to bring balance to the world. And I will not carry this burden alone. I will trust in my allies, in the forces of light, and in the wisdom you have given me."

The spirits of the ancestors nodded in approval, their forms shimmering with a light that seemed to grow brighter as they acknowledged Eryndor's resolve.

"Then go forth, Chosen One," the warrior spirit said, his voice filled with a sense of finality. "Return to the physical world and fulfill your destiny. The path ahead will be difficult, but you are not alone. We will be with you, guiding you, watching over you. And when the time comes, you will know what you must do."

Eryndor bowed their head in gratitude, feeling the weight of the prophecy begin to lift as they accepted the wisdom of their ancestors. They had come seeking guidance, and they had found it—along with a deeper understanding of their role in the prophecy.

The light around them began to fade, the forms of the spirits dissolving into mist as the spirit realm slowly receded. Eryndor felt themselves being drawn back to the physical world, the power of the ley lines guiding them home.

The Return to the Physical World

ERYNDOR AWOKE TO FIND themselves once again kneeling before the altar in the Sacred Grove. The night was still, the air cool and filled with the scent of the forest. The Sword of Legends lay on the stone altar, its blade glowing softly in the moonlight, as if it too had been touched by the wisdom of the ancestors.

For a moment, Eryndor remained kneeling, their mind racing as they processed everything they had experienced in the spirit realm. The guidance of the ancestors had given them a new perspective, a deeper understanding of the prophecy and their role within it. They felt a sense of peace, of clarity, that had eluded them for so long.

Rising to their feet, Eryndor took up the Sword of Legends and held it before them, feeling the weight of the blade in their hands. The sword had been with them since the beginning of their journey, a symbol of their destiny and the power they wielded. But now, it was more than just a weapon—it was a reminder of the balance they needed to bring to the world, of the responsibility they carried as the Chosen One.

As they left the Sacred Grove and made their way back to the encampment, Eryndor felt a renewed sense of purpose. The path ahead would not be easy—there would be more battles, more sacrifices, and more challenges to overcome. But they were ready. The wisdom of the ancestors had given them the strength to continue, to face whatever the future held with courage and determination.

When they arrived at the encampment, they found the Fallen waiting for them. Kael, Lyra, Torin, and Elara all looked relieved to see Eryndor, their faces filled with concern but also with trust. They had seen Eryndor leave for the Sacred Grove and had known that something important was about to happen.

"Eryndor," Kael said, his voice steady. "Did you find what you were looking for?"

Eryndor nodded, their expression calm but resolute. "I did. The ancestors have given me guidance, and I understand now what I must do."

Elara stepped forward, her eyes filled with a sense of understanding. "The spirit realm is a place of great power. What did the ancestors tell you?"

"They told me that the prophecy is not set in stone," Eryndor replied, their voice steady. "It is a path, but the choices we make along the way will shape its outcome. Our role is to bring balance, to guide the forces of light and darkness into alignment so that the world can be saved."

Lyra nodded, her expression thoughtful. "Balance... that makes sense. The enemy is powerful because they've upset the balance of the world. If we can restore that balance, we can weaken them, turn the tide of the war."

Torin looked at Eryndor, his gaze filled with determination. "We're with you, Eryndor. Whatever it takes, we'll see this through together."

Eryndor felt a surge of gratitude and trust in their comrades. The path ahead was uncertain, but they knew that they did not have to walk it alone. The Fallen, the allied forces, the spirits of the ancestors—they were all part of this journey, and together, they would fulfill the prophecy.

"We'll need to act carefully," Eryndor said, their mind already turning to the next steps. "The enemy is still strong, and they'll be looking for any opportunity to exploit our weaknesses. But with the guidance of the ancestors and the strength of our allies, we can bring balance to the world. We can win this war."

The Fallen nodded in agreement, their resolve unwavering. They had faced countless challenges together, and they would face whatever came next with the same determination.

As the night wore on and the stars began to fade from the sky, Eryndor felt a sense of peace settle over them. The prophecy was still a daunting force, but it was no longer a source of fear. It was a guide, a path that they could shape with their actions, their choices.

And as long as they remained true to themselves, true to the balance they sought to bring, they knew that they could fulfill their destiny as the Chosen One.

The spirits of the ancestors had given them the wisdom they needed, and now, it was time to act.

END OF CHAPTER 10

Chapter 11: The Trial of the Hero

The Gathering Storm

The battle against the forces of darkness had been long and arduous, with each victory coming at great cost. But the fall of Eldoria, the guidance of the ancestors, and the realization of the true nature of the prophecy had all led Eryndor to a critical juncture. They knew that their journey was nearing its climax, that the fate of the world hinged on their ability to fulfill their role as the Chosen One.

But before they could face the final confrontation with the enemy, there was one more challenge they had to overcome—one last trial that would determine their worthiness to wield the power necessary to bring balance to the world. This trial, known as the Trial of the Hero, was a test of both physical prowess and inner strength. It was a trial that would push Eryndor to their limits, forcing them to confront not only external threats but also the darkness within themselves.

The Trial of the Hero was a legend among those who knew of the prophecy, whispered about in the ancient texts and passed down through the generations. It was said that only the most worthy, the most determined, could survive the trial and emerge as true heroes. The trial was not just a test of skill in battle—it was a test of character, of morality, and of the very essence of what it meant to be a hero.

The trial was to take place in a mystical realm, a place outside of time and space where the boundaries between reality and illusion blurred. This realm, known as the Vale of Shadows, was a place of immense power, but also immense danger. It was said that those who entered the Vale would face their deepest fears, their darkest desires, and the full weight of their responsibilities. Only by overcoming these challenges could they prove themselves worthy of their destiny.

As the time for the trial approached, Eryndor prepared themselves for the journey to the Vale of Shadows. The night before they were to depart, they gathered with the Fallen—Kael, Lyra, Torin, and Elara—who had been their steadfast companions throughout their journey.

The campfire crackled softly in the cool night air, the flames casting flickering shadows across the faces of the group. The mood was somber but resolute, each of them aware of the importance of the trial that lay ahead.

"You've come so far, Eryndor," Kael said, his deep voice filled with quiet pride. "We've seen you grow into a leader, into the Chosen One the prophecy foretold. But this trial... it's unlike anything we've faced before."

Lyra nodded, her sharp eyes reflecting the firelight. "The Vale of Shadows is a place of great power, but also great danger. It will test you in ways that no battlefield ever could. But I believe in you. We all do."

Torin, ever the practical one, added, "Remember, this isn't just about strength or skill. The Vale will challenge your heart, your mind, and your soul. Stay true to yourself, and you'll make it through."

Elara, her voice soft but filled with conviction, spoke last. "The spirits of the ancestors will be with you, Eryndor. You are not alone, even in the Vale. Trust in the guidance they have given you, and in the strength you've gained along this journey."

Eryndor looked at their friends, their comrades, and felt a swell of gratitude and determination. The path ahead was uncertain, but they knew that they could face it, with the wisdom and strength they had gained from those who had stood by their side.

"I will not fail," Eryndor said, their voice steady. "I will prove myself worthy of the prophecy, worthy of the power needed to bring balance to the world. Thank you all for standing by me, for believing in me. Whatever happens in the Vale, know that I carry your strength with me."

With those words, they spent the rest of the evening in quiet reflection, each of them aware that the dawn would bring the beginning of the final trial.

The Journey to the Vale of Shadows

AS THE FIRST LIGHT of dawn broke over the horizon, Eryndor set out for the Vale of Shadows. The journey took them deep into the heart of the Sacred Grove, past the ancient trees and the ley lines that crisscrossed the land. The path was narrow and winding, the air thick with magic that seemed to hum with anticipation.

Eryndor walked alone, the Sword of Legends strapped to their back, its weight a comforting presence. The sword had been their companion throughout their journey, a symbol of their destiny and the power they wielded. But in the Vale of Shadows, the sword would be more than just a weapon—it would be a key, a conduit for the power that they would need to unlock.

The path led them to a clearing at the edge of the grove, where a shimmering portal hung in the air, its surface rippling like water. This was the entrance to the Vale of Shadows, the gateway to the mystical realm where the trial would take place.

Eryndor paused for a moment, taking a deep breath as they prepared to step through the portal. The air around the portal was cool, a gentle breeze brushing against their skin as they gazed into the swirling depths of the Vale. They knew that once they stepped through, there would be no turning back. The trial would begin, and they would have to face whatever challenges awaited them on the other side.

With a final, resolute nod, Eryndor stepped forward and passed through the portal.

The world around them shifted, the light dimming as they were pulled into the Vale of Shadows. The sensation was disorienting, as if they were being stretched and compressed at the same time, their surroundings a blur of light and shadow.

And then, just as suddenly as it had begun, the sensation stopped.

Eryndor found themselves standing in a vast, mist-shrouded landscape, the ground beneath their feet soft and yielding like the surface of a dream. The air was thick with fog, the sky above a swirling mass of clouds that glowed faintly with an ethereal light. The atmosphere was otherworldly, a place where time and space seemed to lose their meaning.

The Vale of Shadows was both familiar and alien, a place that felt like it existed at the edge of reality. It was a realm of contrasts, where light and darkness coexisted in a delicate balance, where the boundaries between the physical and the spiritual were blurred.

Eryndor looked around, their senses heightened as they took in their surroundings. There was a stillness to the Vale, a silence that felt almost oppressive, as if the very air was holding its breath. But beneath that silence, there was a sense of anticipation, a feeling that something was watching, waiting for them to take the next step.

The Sword of Legends hummed faintly at their side, its power resonating with the energy of the Vale. Eryndor knew that the trial had already begun, that every step they took in this realm would be a test of their resolve, their strength, and their worthiness.

With a deep breath, Eryndor began to walk forward, the mist swirling around them as they made their way deeper into the Vale. The path ahead was unclear, the fog obscuring their vision and making it difficult to see more than a few feet in front of them. But Eryndor knew that they had to keep moving, to push forward and face whatever challenges awaited them.

As they walked, the landscape began to shift and change. The ground beneath their feet grew firmer, the fog thinning as the outlines of structures began to emerge from the mist. Eryndor could see the faint shapes of ancient ruins, crumbling stone walls and pillars that had once stood tall but were now half-buried in the earth. The ruins were a reminder of a time long past, a world that had once been but was now lost to history.

Eryndor continued forward, the ruins growing more defined as they approached. The mist cleared enough for them to see that they were standing at the entrance to a massive temple, its walls carved with intricate patterns and symbols that glowed faintly with a soft, blue light. The temple seemed to pulse with energy, as if it were alive, and Eryndor could feel the power that radiated from its ancient stones.

This was the first trial.

The Trial of the Temple

ERYNDOR STEPPED THROUGH the massive stone archway that marked the entrance to the temple, the air inside cool and heavy with the scent of ancient stone. The temple was vast, its ceiling high above, supported by massive columns that stretched into the darkness. The walls were adorned with carvings and murals that depicted scenes of battles, of heroes and monsters, of light and darkness locked in an eternal struggle.

As Eryndor moved deeper into the temple, the carvings on the walls began to glow with a soft, blue light, casting an eerie glow over the stone floor. The light seemed to follow them, illuminating their path as they made their way through the temple's corridors.

The further they went, the more they could feel the weight of the trial pressing down on them. The temple was a place of power, a place where the boundaries between the physical and the spiritual worlds were thin. It was as if the very stones of the temple were watching, waiting to see if Eryndor was truly worthy.

At the end of the corridor, Eryndor came to a large, circular chamber. The walls were lined with more carvings, and in the center of the chamber stood a massive stone pedestal. Upon the pedestal rested a crystal sphere, its surface smooth and clear, but within it swirled a tempest of light and shadow.

This was the heart of the temple, the source of its power. Eryndor approached the pedestal, their eyes fixed on the crystal sphere. They could feel the energy radiating from it, a pulsing rhythm that seemed to resonate with their own heartbeat.

But as they reached out to touch the sphere, a voice echoed through the chamber, deep and resonant, filling the space with its power.

"Who are you, who dares to seek the power of the ancients?" the voice demanded, its tone commanding and filled with authority.

Eryndor paused, their hand hovering above the sphere. They knew that this was part of the trial, that they would need to prove themselves worthy to the temple and to the power it held.

"I am Eryndor, the Chosen One," they replied, their voice steady. "I seek the power of the ancients to fulfill my destiny, to bring balance to the world and to defeat the darkness that threatens us all."

The voice was silent for a moment, as if considering Eryndor's words. Then it spoke again, its tone measured and deliberate.

"Many have come before you, seeking the power of the ancients. But few have been found worthy. The power you seek is not just for those who are strong of body, but also those who are strong of heart and mind. The trials you will face are not just physical, but also moral. You will be tested, Chosen One, and only if you prove yourself worthy in all aspects will you be granted the power you seek."

Eryndor nodded, understanding the gravity of the trial. They had expected this, but hearing it spoken aloud made it all the more real.

"I am ready," they said, their voice filled with determination. "I will face whatever trials you set before me."

The voice was silent again, and then, with a rumble that seemed to shake the very foundations of the temple, the crystal sphere began to glow brighter, the tempest within it swirling more violently.

"Very well," the voice said, its tone solemn. "Your trial begins now."

The chamber around Eryndor began to shift and change, the walls dissolving into mist as the ground beneath their feet grew unstable. The light from the crystal sphere intensified, enveloping Eryndor in a blinding brilliance.

And then, everything went dark.

The Trial of the Mind

WHEN THE LIGHT FADED, Eryndor found themselves standing in a completely different place. The temple was gone, replaced by a vast, barren landscape. The ground was cracked and dry, the sky above a sickly shade of yellow, the air thick with the stench of decay.

Eryndor looked around, their heart pounding in their chest. This was no ordinary place—it was a realm of the mind, a place where reality and illusion were one and the same. They knew that the trial they now faced was not just physical, but a test of their will, their morality, and their ability to discern truth from falsehood.

As they took a step forward, the ground beneath them cracked and split open, revealing a chasm of darkness that seemed to stretch down into infinity.

Eryndor jumped back, their heart racing as they realized how close they had come to falling into the abyss.

"Do you see, Chosen One?" the voice from the temple echoed around them, its tone both commanding and challenging. "The path before you is treacherous, filled with dangers both seen and unseen. You must tread carefully, for one wrong step could lead to your downfall."

Eryndor nodded, steeling themselves for what lay ahead. They knew that the trial was designed to test their resolve, to push them to their limits. But they also knew that they could not let fear or doubt cloud their judgment.

As they continued forward, the landscape around them began to shift and change. The barren wasteland transformed into a dense forest, the trees towering above them, their branches intertwining to form a thick canopy that blocked out the sky. The air was heavy with the scent of damp earth and rotting leaves, and the sound of rustling branches filled the silence.

Eryndor moved cautiously through the forest, their senses on high alert. They could feel the presence of something watching them, something that moved through the shadows just beyond their sight. But no matter how hard they tried, they could not see it.

Suddenly, a figure emerged from the shadows, stepping into the path before Eryndor. It was a man, tall and gaunt, his face pale and drawn, his eyes hollow and filled with sorrow. He wore tattered robes, his hands trembling as he held out a small, glowing orb.

"Please," the man said, his voice weak and filled with desperation. "Please, take this. It is the last light I have, the last hope I can offer. But I am too weak to carry it any further. Please, take it and use it to bring light to the darkness."

Eryndor hesitated, their hand reaching out to take the orb. But something in the man's eyes gave them pause. There was a shadow behind those eyes, a flicker of something dark and malevolent.

"Why can't you carry it yourself?" Eryndor asked, their voice cautious.

The man's expression faltered for a moment, his eyes narrowing slightly before he forced a smile. "I am too weak," he repeated, his voice wavering. "The darkness has taken too much from me. But you are strong—you can carry it where I cannot."

Eryndor's instincts were screaming at them to be careful, to trust their gut. They could sense that something was not right, that this man was not what he seemed.

"What is this light?" Eryndor asked, their hand lowering slightly. "Why is it so important?"

The man's smile faltered again, his eyes darkening with frustration. "It is hope," he said, his voice growing more insistent. "The only hope that remains in this world. If you do not take it, the darkness will consume everything. You must take it!"

Eryndor took a step back, their eyes narrowing as they studied the man more closely. The orb in his hands was glowing brightly, but there was something off about it, something that seemed almost too perfect, too pristine.

And then they realized—this was a test. The man, the orb, the entire scenario—it was all part of the trial, a challenge designed to test their judgment, their ability to see through deception.

"I cannot take this light," Eryndor said firmly, their voice steady. "For it is not mine to take. If it is truly hope, then it must come from within, not from something outside. This is not real."

The man's eyes flashed with anger, his form shimmering for a moment before dissolving into darkness. The orb in his hands flickered and vanished, leaving nothing but a void where he had stood.

"Well done, Chosen One," the voice from the temple echoed once more, its tone approving. "You have passed the first test. But the trial is far from over. You must continue to prove your worthiness, not just through your strength, but through your wisdom and your heart."

The forest around Eryndor began to shift and change again, the trees melting away into mist as the landscape transformed once more. This time, they found themselves standing on the edge of a cliff, the ground falling away into a deep, dark abyss below. The sky above was filled with swirling clouds, the wind howling around them like a living thing.

Eryndor took a step forward, the wind tugging at their clothes and threatening to pull them over the edge. They could feel the power of the Vale of Shadows all around them, the very air charged with energy. But they also knew that they could not falter now—they had to continue, to face whatever challenges lay ahead.

As they stood at the edge of the cliff, a figure emerged from the swirling mist. It was a woman, her hair long and flowing, her eyes filled with a deep sadness. She was dressed in a simple gown, her hands clasped in front of her as she looked out over the abyss.

"You are the Chosen One," the woman said, her voice soft but filled with a quiet strength. "But you are also just one person, one soul in a world filled with many. How can you carry the weight of the world on your shoulders? How can you bear the burden of the prophecy, knowing that your choices will shape the fate of so many?"

Eryndor felt a pang of doubt, the woman's words striking at the heart of their deepest fears. They had always known that their role was important, but hearing it spoken aloud made the weight of their responsibility all the more real.

"I don't know," Eryndor admitted, their voice filled with uncertainty. "But I have to try. I have to do whatever it takes to fulfill the prophecy, to bring balance to the world."

The woman nodded, her expression compassionate. "But what if you fail? What if the burden becomes too much? What if you make the wrong choices, and the world is lost because of you?"

Eryndor felt the weight of those questions pressing down on them, the doubt and fear growing stronger with each passing moment. But they also knew that this was another test, a challenge to their resolve.

"I will do my best," Eryndor said, their voice firm. "I cannot promise that I will not make mistakes, or that I will always know the right path. But I can promise that I will never give up, that I will continue to fight for what is right, no matter how difficult the journey becomes."

The woman smiled, her sadness lifting slightly. "That is all anyone can ask of you, Chosen One. To try, to fight, to never give up. Remember that the true strength of a hero is not just in their ability to win battles, but in their ability to keep going, even when the odds are against them."

With those words, the woman dissolved into mist, leaving Eryndor standing alone on the edge of the cliff. The wind around them began to calm, the swirling clouds above parting to reveal a clear sky filled with stars.

"You have done well, Chosen One," the voice from the temple said, its tone filled with approval. "You have passed the second test. But there is one final challenge you must face before you can claim the power of the ancients."

The ground beneath Eryndor's feet began to shift, the cliff dissolving into mist as the landscape transformed once more. This time, they found themselves standing in a familiar place—the battlefield where they had fought their first major battle against the forces of darkness.

The ground was littered with the bodies of fallen soldiers, the air thick with the stench of blood and death. The sky above was dark and foreboding, filled with storm clouds that rumbled ominously.

Eryndor looked around, their heart heavy as they took in the sight of the battlefield. This was a place of pain and loss, a reminder of the cost of the war they were fighting. But it was also a place of courage and sacrifice, a place where they had fought alongside their comrades to protect what they held dear.

As they stood there, the ground began to tremble, the air growing thick with tension. Eryndor could feel the presence of something powerful, something that was watching them, waiting to strike.

And then, from the shadows, a figure emerged.

It was a warrior, clad in dark armor, their face hidden behind a helmet. They carried a massive sword, its blade crackling with dark energy. The warrior's presence was overwhelming, a force of pure malevolence that seemed to radiate from their very being.

This was the final trial.

The Trial of the Body

THE DARK WARRIOR STEPPED forward, their movements slow and deliberate, each step causing the ground to tremble beneath their feet. Eryndor could feel the power radiating from the warrior, a cold, oppressive energy that seemed to sap the strength from their limbs.

The warrior raised their sword, pointing it directly at Eryndor. "You are the Chosen One," the warrior said, their voice deep and filled with malice. "But you are also just a mortal, bound by the limitations of flesh and blood. You may have passed the trials of the mind and heart, but now you must face the trial of the body. Only by defeating me will you prove yourself truly worthy of the power you seek."

Eryndor's grip tightened on the hilt of the Sword of Legends, their resolve hardening. They knew that this was the final test, the ultimate challenge that would determine whether they were truly worthy of the prophecy.

The warrior lunged forward, their massive sword slashing through the air with a speed that belied its size. Eryndor barely had time to react, raising their sword to block the attack. The force of the blow sent them stumbling back, their arms aching from the impact.

The dark warrior pressed the attack, their strikes relentless and powerful. Each blow seemed to grow stronger, the dark energy of the warrior's sword crackling with malevolent power. Eryndor struggled to keep up, their body pushed to its limits as they parried and dodged each strike.

But the trial was not just a test of strength—it was a test of endurance, of willpower, of the ability to keep fighting even when the odds were against them. Eryndor knew that they could not afford to falter, that they had to find a way to overcome the dark warrior's power.

Summoning every ounce of strength and determination, Eryndor launched a counterattack. The Sword of Legends blazed with light, its power resonating with the energy of the Vale of Shadows. Eryndor's strikes were swift and precise, each one aimed at finding a weakness in the warrior's defenses.

The battle raged on, the clash of swords echoing across the battlefield. Eryndor could feel the strain on their body, their muscles burning with fatigue, but they refused to give up. The words of the ancestors echoed in their mind, reminding them that true strength came from within, from the will to keep fighting even when all seemed lost.

With a final, desperate surge of energy, Eryndor managed to land a decisive blow. The Sword of Legends sliced through the dark warrior's armor, striking at the heart of the malevolent energy that fueled them.

The warrior staggered back, their sword falling from their grasp as they clutched at the wound. The dark energy around them began to dissipate, the malevolent power fading as the warrior's form began to shimmer and dissolve.

Eryndor stood tall, their chest heaving with exertion, but their resolve unbroken. They had passed the trial of the body, proving their strength and their worthiness to wield the power of the ancients.

The battlefield around them began to fade, the storm clouds parting as the light of the Vale of Shadows returned. The voice from the temple echoed one final time, its tone filled with pride and approval.

"You have passed the final trial, Chosen One. You have proven yourself worthy of the power of the ancients. Go forth, and fulfill your destiny."

The light of the Vale enveloped Eryndor, lifting them from the battlefield and carrying them back to the physical world. The trial was over, and they had emerged victorious.

The Return to the Physical World

ERYNDOR AWOKE TO FIND themselves back in the Sacred Grove, kneeling before the altar where the trial had begun. The Sword of Legends lay across their lap, its blade glowing softly with the power they had gained from the Vale of Shadows.

The air around them was calm and still, the grove filled with the soft sounds of nature. The weight of the trial was still heavy on their shoulders, but it was now tempered by a sense of accomplishment, of fulfillment. They had passed the Trial of the Hero, and in doing so, they had proven themselves worthy of the prophecy.

As they rose to their feet, Eryndor felt a deep sense of peace, of clarity. The trial had tested them in every way possible—physically, mentally, and emotionally. But they had faced each challenge with courage and determination, and they had emerged stronger for it.

The wisdom of the ancestors, the strength of the Sword of Legends, and the power of the Vale of Shadows were now all a part of them, a part of their journey. They were ready to face whatever challenges lay ahead, to fulfill their destiny and bring balance to the world.

As they made their way back to the encampment, Eryndor knew that the final battle was drawing near. The enemy was still out there, still waiting, but they were no longer afraid. They had faced the darkness within themselves, and they had triumphed.

The Trial of the Hero was over, but the true test—the battle to save the world—was yet to come.

But Eryndor was ready. They were the Chosen One, and they would fulfill their destiny.

End of Chapter 11

Chapter 12: The Alliance of the Kingdoms

The Aftermath of the Trials

The Trial of the Hero had left Eryndor not only physically exhausted but also deeply introspective. The insights gained from their journey through the Vale of Shadows lingered in their mind, shaping their thoughts and strategies. As the Chosen One, they were now more certain of their role in the prophecy than ever before, but they also knew that the battle ahead could not be won through individual strength alone. The time had come to unite the world against the looming darkness.

The enemy's advance was relentless, their forces growing stronger with each passing day. The fall of Eldoria had sent shockwaves through the allied forces, and despite their best efforts to regroup and fortify their positions, the specter of defeat hung heavily over them. Eryndor knew that without a significant shift in power, the battle against the darkness could be lost.

In the days following the trial, as they recuperated in the Sacred Grove, Eryndor began to formulate a plan—one that required more than just the forces they had at their disposal. The prophecy spoke of a hero who would unite the world, and Eryndor realized that this unity was not just a symbolic gesture; it was a strategic necessity. If the forces of light were to stand a chance against the enemy, they needed more than just strength; they needed numbers, resources, and the combined might of all the kingdoms.

But the path to unity was fraught with challenges. The kingdoms of the world had long been divided by rivalries, grudges, and deep-seated animosities. Eryndor knew that convincing them to set aside their differences and join forces would require more than just words—it would require diplomacy, negotiation, and, most importantly, sacrifice.

The Call to Diplomacy

ERYNDOR GATHERED THE Fallen—Kael, Lyra, Torin, and Elara—for a council in the heart of the Sacred Grove. The atmosphere was tense but hopeful, each of them aware that the decisions made in this council could determine the fate of the world.

"We cannot win this war alone," Eryndor began, their voice steady but firm. "The prophecy has guided us this far, but it has also shown me that unity is our greatest strength. The enemy's power grows with each passing day, and if we are to defeat them, we must unite the kingdoms."

Kael nodded, his expression thoughtful. "The kingdoms have always been wary of one another. There's been too much bloodshed, too many old wounds. But if we can bring them together, if we can convince them that this is a battle for the survival of all, then maybe we have a chance."

Lyra, ever the strategist, added, "We'll need to approach this carefully. Each kingdom has its own interests, its own fears. We have to make them see that their best chance for survival lies in unity. But we also need to be prepared to make concessions, to give them something in return for their allegiance."

Torin, his fiery spirit tempered by the gravity of the situation, spoke next. "We'll also need to show them that we're serious about this alliance. A show of strength, a demonstration of our commitment to the cause. If they see that we're willing to fight, to sacrifice, they might be more inclined to join us."

Elara, her eyes distant as she gazed into the future, finally spoke. "I've seen glimpses of what could be—a great alliance, stronger than any force the world has ever known. But I've also seen the dangers, the challenges that lie ahead. This won't be easy, Eryndor. The kingdoms are proud, stubborn. Convincing them to unite will be the greatest challenge we've faced yet."

Eryndor listened to their comrades, their mind already racing with ideas and strategies. They knew that the task ahead would not be easy, but they also knew that it was the only way forward. The enemy was too powerful, too entrenched. Only by uniting the kingdoms could they hope to turn the tide of the war.

"We'll begin with those who are closest to us," Eryndor decided. "The Kingdom of Thaloria, the elves of Valandor, and the dwarves of Stonehelm. They've been our allies before, and they have the most to lose if the enemy prevails. If we can secure their support, it will give us a strong foundation to build upon."

The Fallen agreed, and plans were set in motion. Messages were sent to the leaders of Thaloria, Valandor, and Stonehelm, requesting urgent meetings to discuss a matter of the utmost importance. Eryndor knew that these first negotiations would set the tone for the rest of their diplomatic efforts, and they were determined to make them count.

The Kingdom of Thaloria

THE FIRST STOP ON ERYNDOR'S diplomatic journey was the Kingdom of Thaloria, a land of rolling hills, dense forests, and ancient castles. Thaloria had long been a stronghold of the forces of light, its armies renowned for their skill in battle and their unwavering loyalty to the cause. But the kingdom had also suffered greatly in the war, its borders constantly under threat from the enemy's forces.

Eryndor and the Fallen were received with great ceremony at the royal palace, a sprawling fortress of stone and iron that had stood for centuries. King Aldric, a stern and battle-hardened ruler, welcomed them into his council chamber, where the banners of Thaloria hung proudly from the walls.

"Eryndor," King Aldric greeted them, his voice gruff but respectful. "It is good to see you again. I wish it were under better circumstances."

"As do I, Your Majesty," Eryndor replied, bowing respectfully. "But the situation has grown dire, and I fear that we have little time to waste. The enemy grows stronger with each passing day, and I believe that the only way to defeat them is through a united front—a grand alliance of all the kingdoms."

King Aldric frowned, his brow furrowing as he considered Eryndor's words. "A united front? You speak of an alliance, but Thaloria has always stood alone, proud and independent. Why should we ally ourselves with those who have never lifted a finger to help us in our time of need?"

Eryndor expected this reaction. Thaloria's history was one of fierce independence, its people proud of their ability to defend their land without relying on others. But they also knew that appealing to King Aldric's sense of duty and pragmatism would be key.

"Because the enemy we face now is unlike any we have fought before," Eryndor replied, their voice filled with conviction. "They are not just a threat to Thaloria, but to the entire world. If they succeed, there will be no kingdom left to stand alone. We must unite, not out of weakness, but out of strength. Together, we can stand against the darkness and protect everything we hold dear."

King Aldric's expression softened slightly, but he remained cautious. "And what of the other kingdoms? What guarantee do we have that they will honor this alliance? Thaloria has been betrayed before, Eryndor. I will not see my people suffer for the mistakes of others."

Eryndor nodded, understanding the king's concerns. "I cannot offer you guarantees, Your Majesty, but I can offer you my word. I will not rest until this alliance is secured, until every kingdom stands together against the enemy. I ask for your trust, not just in me, but in the prophecy that has guided us this far. We have a chance to turn the tide of this war, but only if we stand united."

King Aldric studied Eryndor for a long moment, his gaze searching. Finally, he nodded slowly, a hint of a smile tugging at the corners of his lips.

"You have always been a persuasive one, Eryndor," the king said, his tone warming. "Very well. Thaloria will join this alliance. But know this—I expect loyalty and honor from our allies. If they betray us, there will be consequences."

Eryndor bowed deeply, grateful for the king's support. "Thank you, Your Majesty. Together, we will ensure that the light prevails."

With Thaloria's support secured, Eryndor and the Fallen left the royal palace with a renewed sense of purpose. They knew that this was just the first step, but it was an important one. Thaloria's armies were strong, and their participation in the alliance would lend credibility to the cause.

The next stop was Valandor, the kingdom of the elves.

The Elves of Valandor

VALANDOR WAS A LAND of unparalleled beauty, its forests lush and vibrant, its cities built seamlessly into the natural landscape. The elves of Valandor were a proud and ancient people, known for their wisdom, their skill in magic, and their deep connection to the natural world. But they were also wary of outsiders, their long history of isolation making them cautious in their dealings with other kingdoms.

Eryndor and the Fallen were met at the borders of Valandor by a delegation of elven warriors, their armor gleaming in the sunlight, their bows and swords at the ready. They were escorted through the forest to the capital city of Aeloria, a breathtaking metropolis where trees and buildings blended together in perfect harmony.

The elven king, Aerandir, was a regal figure, his silver hair flowing down his back, his eyes sharp and discerning. He received Eryndor and the Fallen in the Hall of the Ancients, a grand chamber filled with the echoes of Valandor's long and storied past.

"Eryndor," King Aerandir greeted them, his voice smooth and melodic. "You have come to Valandor in a time of great need. The trees whisper of war, and the winds carry the scent of darkness. What brings you to our land?"

Eryndor bowed respectfully. "Your Majesty, I come seeking your aid. The enemy we face is powerful, and their influence spreads far and wide. They threaten not just the human kingdoms, but all life in this world. We seek to form an alliance, a united front against the darkness, and we ask for Valandor's support."

King Aerandir's expression was contemplative, his gaze distant as he considered Eryndor's words. "The elves of Valandor have long stood apart from the affairs of the human kingdoms. We are guardians of the natural world, protectors of the ancient ways. Why should we entangle ourselves in the conflicts of others?"

Eryndor knew that appealing to the elves' sense of duty to the natural world would be key to gaining their support. The elves had always seen themselves as the caretakers of the earth, and the destruction wrought by the enemy was a direct threat to everything they held dear.

"Because the darkness we face now threatens the very fabric of the world," Eryndor replied, their voice filled with urgency. "The enemy seeks to corrupt and destroy everything that is pure, everything that is good. The forests, the rivers, the mountains—all will fall if we do not stand against them. Valandor's wisdom and strength are needed now more than ever. If we unite, we can protect the natural world and ensure that the beauty of Valandor endures."

King Aerandir's eyes narrowed slightly, but there was a spark of interest in his gaze. "You speak with passion, Eryndor, and I can sense the truth in your words. But an alliance is not a simple matter. The elves have seen many betrayals in our long history, and we do not trust easily. What assurances can you give us that this alliance will be honored?"

Eryndor took a deep breath, knowing that this was the moment to appeal to the king's sense of honor and duty. "Your Majesty, I can offer you no guarantees, only my word and my commitment to the cause. But I ask you to consider the greater good. This alliance is not just about survival—it is about preserving the balance of the world, about protecting the natural order. Valandor's place in this alliance is not just as a participant, but as a leader, a beacon of hope for all who seek to protect the earth."

King Aerandir was silent for a long moment, his gaze locked on Eryndor's. Finally, he nodded, his expression softening.

"Very well, Eryndor," the king said, his voice carrying a note of finality. "Valandor will join your alliance. We will stand with you against the darkness, not just for the sake of the world, but for the sake of all that we hold dear. But know this—the elves do not fight for glory or power. We fight to protect the earth, and we expect the same commitment from our allies."

Eryndor bowed deeply, grateful for the king's support. "Thank you, Your Majesty. Together, we will ensure that the light prevails."

With Valandor's support secured, Eryndor and the Fallen left Aeloria with a sense of accomplishment. The elves' participation in the alliance was a significant victory, as their wisdom, magic, and connection to the natural world would be invaluable in the battles to come.

The next stop was Stonehelm, the kingdom of the dwarves.

The Dwarves of Stonehelm

STONEHELM WAS A KINGDOM built deep within the mountains, its cities carved into the living rock, its halls filled with the sound of hammers striking anvils. The dwarves of Stonehelm were known for their craftsmanship, their skill in battle, and their stubbornness. They were a proud people, fiercely independent and often wary of outsiders.

Eryndor and the Fallen were met at the gates of Stonehelm by a group of dwarven warriors, their armor heavy and ornate, their axes sharp and ready. They were escorted into the heart of the mountain, where the great halls of Stonehelm echoed with the sound of industry.

The dwarven king, Thrain Ironfist, was a burly figure, his beard long and braided, his eyes sharp and shrewd. He received Eryndor and the Fallen in the Hall of Kings, a vast chamber filled with the statues of dwarven heroes and ancestors.

"Eryndor," King Thrain greeted them, his voice booming through the hall. "It's been a long time since a human has set foot in Stonehelm. What brings you to our kingdom?"

Eryndor bowed respectfully. "Your Majesty, I come seeking your aid. The enemy we face is powerful, and their influence spreads far and wide. They threaten not just the human kingdoms, but all life in this world. We seek to form an alliance, a united front against the darkness, and we ask for Stonehelm's support."

King Thrain's expression was guarded, his gaze piercing as he considered Eryndor's words. "An alliance, you say? Stonehelm has always stood on its own, strong and unyielding. We've weathered many storms, and we've always come out stronger. Why should we ally ourselves with those who may not have the same strength?"

Eryndor knew that appealing to the dwarves' sense of honor and strength would be key to gaining their support. The dwarves had always prided themselves on their resilience, their ability to stand firm in the face of adversity.

"Because the enemy we face now is unlike any we have fought before," Eryndor replied, their voice steady and confident. "They are not just a threat to Stonehelm, but to the entire world. They seek to corrupt and destroy everything that is good, everything that is strong. Stonehelm's strength is needed now more than ever. If we unite, we can stand firm against the darkness and protect everything we hold dear."

King Thrain's eyes narrowed slightly, but there was a hint of respect in his gaze. "You speak of strength, but strength alone is not enough to win a war. What else do you offer in this alliance?"

Eryndor took a deep breath, knowing that this was the moment to appeal to the king's sense of honor and duty. "Your Majesty, I offer you the strength of unity. Together, the kingdoms of the world can stand against the darkness, can protect the light. I offer you the wisdom of the elves, the courage of the humans, and the strength of the dwarves. Together, we can ensure that the light prevails."

King Thrain was silent for a long moment, his gaze locked on Eryndor's. Finally, he nodded, his expression softening.

"Very well, Eryndor," the king said, his voice carrying a note of finality. "Stonehelm will join your alliance. We will stand with you against the darkness, not just for the sake of the world, but for the sake of all that we hold dear. But know this—the dwarves do not fight for glory or power. We fight to protect our home, and we expect the same commitment from our allies."

Eryndor bowed deeply, grateful for the king's support. "Thank you, Your Majesty. Together, we will ensure that the light prevails."

With Stonehelm's support secured, Eryndor and the Fallen left the kingdom of the dwarves with a sense of accomplishment. The dwarves' participation in the alliance was a significant victory, as their strength, resilience, and craftsmanship would be invaluable in the battles to come.

But the journey was far from over.

The Alliance of the Kingdoms

WITH THE SUPPORT OF Thaloria, Valandor, and Stonehelm secured, Eryndor and the Fallen returned to the Sacred Grove to prepare for the final negotiations. The alliance was beginning to take shape, but there were still many challenges ahead. The kingdoms were proud and independent, and uniting them under a single banner would require careful diplomacy, negotiation, and, most importantly, sacrifice.

Eryndor knew that the alliance would need a strong foundation, a set of principles and agreements that all the kingdoms could agree upon. They spent long hours in council with the Fallen, drafting a treaty that would outline the terms of the alliance, the responsibilities of each kingdom, and the goals they sought to achieve.

The treaty was ambitious, but it was also realistic. It acknowledged the differences between the kingdoms, but it also emphasized the importance of unity and cooperation. It called for shared resources, joint military efforts, and mutual respect. It was a document that Eryndor hoped would bring the kingdoms together, not just as allies, but as partners in the fight against the darkness.

Once the treaty was finalized, Eryndor sent out invitations to the leaders of the remaining kingdoms, asking them to come to the Sacred Grove for a grand council. It was a bold move, but Eryndor knew that if the alliance was to succeed, it needed the support of all the kingdoms.

The response was mixed. Some leaders were eager to join the alliance, recognizing the threat posed by the enemy and the benefits of unity. Others were more hesitant, wary of the implications of such an alliance and the sacrifices it might require.

But in the end, all the invited leaders agreed to attend the council, realizing that the stakes were too high to ignore.

The grand council was held in the Sacred Grove, under the ancient trees that had witnessed countless battles and the rise and fall of empires. The leaders of the kingdoms gathered around a great table, the treaty laid out before them, the air thick with tension and anticipation.

Eryndor stood at the head of the table, their heart pounding with a mix of nerves and determination. This was the moment they had been preparing for, the moment that could determine the fate of the world.

"Honored leaders," Eryndor began, their voice steady but filled with emotion. "We have come together today not as enemies, but as allies. The darkness that threatens us is powerful, and it seeks to destroy everything we hold dear. But together, we can stand against it. Together, we can protect our world, our people, and our future."

The leaders listened in silence, their expressions guarded but attentive. Eryndor knew that they were skeptical, that they had come to the council with their own interests and concerns. But they also knew that the threat of the enemy was real, and that the only way to defeat it was through unity.

"The treaty before you outlines the terms of our alliance," Eryndor continued. "It calls for shared resources, joint military efforts, and mutual respect. It acknowledges our differences, but it also emphasizes the importance of cooperation. This is not just a treaty—it is a promise. A promise to stand together, to fight together, and to protect our world together."

The leaders murmured among themselves, their voices low and cautious. Eryndor could sense their hesitation, their fear of losing their independence, their doubt that such an alliance could succeed.

But they also sensed something else—a glimmer of hope, a recognition that this was their best chance for survival.

King Aldric of Thaloria was the first to speak. "Eryndor is right," he said, his voice firm. "The enemy we face is unlike any we have fought before. They threaten not just Thaloria, but all of us. We must set aside our differences, our old grudges, and unite. Thaloria will honor this treaty, and we will stand with our allies in the fight against the darkness."

King Aerandir of Valandor nodded in agreement. "The elves of Valandor have long stood apart, but we recognize the need for unity in the face of such a threat. We will join this alliance, not just to protect our lands, but to protect the balance of the world."

King Thrain of Stonehelm added his voice. "Stonehelm has always stood strong, and we will continue to do so. But we also know that strength comes from unity. We will join this alliance, and we will fight alongside our allies to protect our home."

One by one, the other leaders spoke, voicing their support for the alliance. Some were more hesitant than others, but in the end, all agreed to sign the treaty, recognizing that the threat of the enemy was too great to ignore.

The treaty was signed with great ceremony, each leader adding their seal to the document, binding their kingdoms to the alliance. It was a moment of triumph, a moment that marked the beginning of a new chapter in the war against the darkness.

With the alliance secured, the united forces began to prepare for the final battle. The armies of the kingdoms mobilized, their soldiers trained and equipped for the coming conflict. Resources were pooled, strategies were devised, and plans were set in motion.

But even as the preparations continued, Eryndor knew that the true test was yet to come. The enemy was powerful, and the final battle would be fierce. But with the alliance of the kingdoms, they had a chance—a chance to turn the tide, to protect the light, and to fulfill the prophecy.

As they stood in the Sacred Grove, surrounded by the leaders of the kingdoms, Eryndor felt a sense of hope, a sense of purpose. The journey had been long and difficult, but they had come this far, and they would not falter now.

The Alliance of the Kingdoms was strong, and together, they would face the darkness.

The final battle was coming, and they were ready.

End of Chapter 12

Chapter 13: The Battle of Blood and Fire

The Calm Before the Storm

The sun rose over the horizon, casting long shadows across the landscape. The Sacred Grove, which had been a sanctuary for Eryndor and the allied forces, was now a place of final preparations. The trees, ancient and wise, seemed to stand in silent witness to the gathering storm. The air was thick with tension, the kind that precedes a great and terrible event, and every warrior present could feel the weight of what was about to unfold.

Eryndor stood at the edge of the grove, overlooking the vast plain where the battle would soon rage. The Sword of Legends hung at their side, its blade gleaming in the early morning light, a reminder of the power they wielded and the responsibility that came with it. The prophecy had brought them to this moment, but it was their own choices, their own courage, that would determine the outcome of the war.

The allied forces had assembled in full strength, a sight to behold. The armies of Thaloria, Valandor, Stonehelm, and the other kingdoms that had joined the alliance stretched as far as the eye could see. Banners of every color fluttered in the breeze, each representing a different kingdom, a different people, all united by the common cause of defeating the darkness.

The elves of Valandor, with their silver armor and graceful weapons, moved with a quiet confidence, their archers readying their bows, their mages preparing powerful spells. The dwarves of Stonehelm, clad in their heavy, ornately crafted armor, stood in tight formations, their axes and hammers gleaming in the light. The soldiers of Thaloria, known for their discipline and bravery, stood at attention, their swords and shields held high, ready to face whatever the enemy would throw at them.

Eryndor's closest companions, the Fallen, were by their side, each prepared for the battle ahead. Kael the Unbroken, his warhammer resting on his shoulder, radiated a quiet strength. Lyra the Shadowblade, her twin daggers sheathed at her side, was a picture of deadly grace. Torin the Flameborn, his hands crackling with barely contained fire magic, exuded fierce determination. Elara the Starseer, her eyes filled with the knowledge of countless visions, was calm and resolute.

They had all come so far, faced so many challenges, and now they stood on the precipice of the final battle. The enemy was out there, somewhere beyond the horizon, gathering their forces, preparing for the confrontation that would decide the fate of the world.

Eryndor felt a hand on their shoulder and turned to see Elara standing beside them, her expression thoughtful.

"The visions have been coming more frequently," Elara said softly, her voice barely audible above the rustle of the wind. "I've seen glimpses of what is to come, but nothing is certain. The future is a shifting tapestry, and the choices we make today will shape its pattern."

Eryndor nodded, understanding the weight of her words. "We've done all we can to prepare. Now, it's up to us—to fight, to endure, and to prevail."

Elara looked out over the plain, her gaze distant. "The battle will be fierce, and the cost will be high. But we must remember why we fight—not just for victory, but for the light, for the hope that still remains."

Eryndor squeezed her hand briefly before turning back to the battlefield. "We fight for a future worth saving. Let's make sure that future comes to pass."

As the morning wore on, the allied forces completed their preparations. Scouts reported back with news of the enemy's approach, and the commanders moved to their positions. The time for battle was drawing near, and the tension in the air was almost palpable.

Eryndor took a deep breath, calming their nerves. They knew that this would be the greatest test they had ever faced, but they also knew that they were not alone. The Sword of Legends pulsed with a faint light, as if sensing the significance of the moment. The power within it was immense, but it was up to Eryndor to wield it wisely, to harness that power for the good of all.

With a final glance at their companions, Eryndor stepped forward, raising the Sword of Legends high above their head. The light of the blade caught the attention of the assembled armies, and a hush fell over the battlefield as all eyes turned to the Chosen One.

"For the light!" Eryndor shouted, their voice ringing out across the plain. "For our future!"

A cheer rose up from the ranks of the allied forces, a sound filled with hope, determination, and a fierce resolve. The time for words was over. The time for action had come.

The First Clash

THE ENEMY EMERGED FROM the mist like a tide of darkness, a vast horde of twisted creatures, corrupted by the malevolent forces that had spawned them. At their head were the dark sorcerers, their hands crackling with forbidden magic, their eyes glowing with an unnatural light. Behind them, massive beasts lumbered forward, their roars echoing across the battlefield, shaking the very earth beneath them.

The two armies stood facing each other, a vast gulf of empty space between them, the silence before the storm. Eryndor could feel the tension in the air, the anticipation of the clash that was about to occur. Every breath seemed to take an eternity, every heartbeat a thunderous drumbeat in their ears.

And then, with a deafening roar, the battle began.

The allied forces surged forward as one, a wave of steel, magic, and determination. The elves of Valandor unleashed a barrage of arrows, their shafts flying with deadly precision, cutting down the front ranks of the enemy. The dwarves of Stonehelm charged into the fray, their axes and hammers smashing through the enemy's lines with brutal force. The soldiers of Thaloria, their swords gleaming, pressed the attack, their shields locked in formation as they pushed forward.

Eryndor led the charge, the Sword of Legends blazing with a light that cut through the darkness like a beacon of hope. They struck down the enemy with every swing, the sword's power searing through the twisted flesh of the creatures that stood in their path. Around them, the battle raged, a cacophony of clashing steel, roaring flames, and the cries of the wounded.

Kael fought beside Eryndor, his warhammer crushing skulls and breaking bones with every swing. He was a force of nature, his presence a rallying point for the soldiers around him. Lyra moved through the shadows, her daggers flashing as she struck down the dark sorcerers who tried to use their magic against the allied forces. Torin unleashed waves of fire, his magic searing through the enemy's ranks, turning the battlefield into an inferno. Elara guided the forces of light, her visions allowing her to anticipate the enemy's movements and to direct the allied forces with precision.

The battle was fierce, the enemy relentless in their assault. But the allied forces fought with a determination born of desperation, knowing that this was their last chance, their final stand against the darkness. The ground beneath them was soon soaked with blood, the air thick with the stench of death and the smoke of battle.

Eryndor fought with everything they had, the Sword of Legends cleaving through the enemy with a power that seemed to grow with each strike. But even as they cut down one foe after another, they knew that this was just the beginning. The true test was yet to come.

The Flames of War

AS THE BATTLE RAGED on, the enemy unleashed their full might, bringing forth their most powerful and terrifying weapons. Massive siege engines, pulled by monstrous beasts, began to hurl flaming boulders into the allied ranks, the impact sending soldiers flying and setting the ground ablaze. The dark sorcerers combined their powers, creating massive storms of fire and lightning that tore through the allied lines, leaving devastation in their wake.

Eryndor could see that the allied forces were beginning to falter under the onslaught. The flames spread quickly, consuming everything in their path, turning the battlefield into a hellish landscape of smoke and fire. The screams of the wounded and dying filled the air, mingling with the roars of the enemy and the thunderous crash of battle.

But even in the face of such destruction, Eryndor refused to give up. They called upon the power of the Sword of Legends, channeling its energy into a protective barrier that shielded the soldiers around them from the flames. The sword's light shone brightly, cutting through the smoke and chaos, giving the allied forces a glimmer of hope.

"Hold the line!" Eryndor shouted, their voice carrying over the roar of the flames. "Do not let them break us!"

Kael, Lyra, Torin, and Elara rallied the soldiers, their presence a source of strength and courage. Kael's warhammer smashed through the enemy's siege engines, his raw power breaking the machines into splinters. Lyra led a group of elite soldiers in a daring raid on the dark sorcerers, striking them down before they could unleash more of their destructive magic. Torin countered the enemy's flames with his own fire magic, creating walls of fire that held back the enemy's advance. Elara used her foresight to guide the soldiers through the chaos, ensuring that they avoided the worst of the enemy's attacks.

But despite their efforts, the enemy's forces were vast and unrelenting. The flames continued to spread, and the allied forces were being pushed back, their lines beginning to crumble under the pressure.

Eryndor knew that they had to act quickly, that they had to find a way to turn the tide of the battle. They could feel the enemy's leader, the source of the darkness, somewhere on the battlefield, watching, waiting. The time had come to face them, to end this once and for all.

With a determined look, Eryndor turned to the Fallen. "It's time. I'm going after the enemy's leader."

Kael nodded, his expression grim. "We'll hold the line here. Go, Eryndor. Finish this."

Lyra placed a hand on Eryndor's arm, her eyes filled with a fierce resolve. "We'll keep them off your back. Just make sure you come back to us."

Torin grinned, his fiery spirit undiminished. "Give them hell, Eryndor."

Elara's gaze was distant, her voice soft but firm. "The path ahead is dangerous, but it is the only way. Trust in the light, Eryndor."

With a final nod to their companions, Eryndor took a deep breath and turned toward the heart of the enemy's forces. The flames roared around them, but the Sword of Legends blazed with a light that cut through the darkness, guiding them forward.

They knew that this was it—the final confrontation, the moment that would decide the fate of the world.

The Duel

ERYNDOR MADE THEIR way through the battlefield, cutting down any enemy that dared to stand in their way. The heat of the flames was intense, the air thick with smoke and ash, but they pressed on, driven by a single purpose. The Sword of Legends pulsed with power, its light growing brighter as they drew closer to the enemy's leader.

Finally, they reached the heart of the enemy's forces, a place where the darkness was so thick that it seemed to choke the very life from the air. There, standing amidst the flames, was the enemy's leader—a towering figure clad in dark armor, their face hidden behind a fearsome helm. In their hand, they held a massive sword, its blade crackling with dark energy.

The leader turned to face Eryndor, their eyes glowing with an unnatural light. The air around them seemed to pulse with malevolent power, the ground beneath their feet blackened and scorched.

"Eryndor, the Chosen One," the leader said, their voice deep and filled with malice. "You've come at last. Do you truly believe you can defeat me? Do you truly believe you can stop the inevitable?"

Eryndor met the leader's gaze, their own eyes filled with determination. "I believe in the light, and I believe in the strength of those who fight for it. This ends here."

The leader laughed, a cold, mocking sound that sent shivers down Eryndor's spine. "Fool. The light is weak, and those who follow it are doomed to fall. The darkness is eternal, and it will consume all."

With a roar, the leader charged at Eryndor, their massive sword swinging in a wide arc. Eryndor barely had time to raise the Sword of Legends to block the attack, the force of the blow sending them stumbling back.

The duel began in earnest, the two combatants clashing with a ferocity that shook the battlefield. The leader's strikes were powerful, each one fueled by the dark energy that radiated from their sword. But Eryndor fought with a determination born of hope, their own sword blazing with a light that pushed back the darkness.

The battle was intense, the two warriors evenly matched. Every strike, every parry, sent shockwaves through the air, the ground trembling beneath their feet. The flames roared around them, a backdrop to their struggle, but neither combatant paid them any mind. Their focus was solely on each other, on the fight that would decide the fate of the world.

Eryndor could feel the strain on their body, the weight of the Sword of Legends growing heavier with each swing. But they refused to give up, refused to let the darkness win. They knew that they had to keep fighting, had to find a way to overcome the enemy's power.

With a sudden burst of energy, Eryndor unleashed a powerful strike, the Sword of Legends glowing with a blinding light as it clashed with the leader's blade. The force of the impact sent a shockwave through the air, the ground cracking beneath their feet.

The leader staggered back, their dark armor cracked and smoking from the force of the blow. For the first time, Eryndor saw a flicker of doubt in their eyes, a crack in their confidence.

"You cannot win," Eryndor said, their voice filled with conviction. "The light is stronger than you know. It cannot be extinguished."

The leader snarled, their eyes blazing with fury. "The light is nothing! I will show you the true power of the darkness!"

With a roar, the leader unleashed a torrent of dark energy, the ground around them erupting in flames and shadows. Eryndor raised the Sword of Legends, its light forming a protective barrier around them as the darkness crashed against it.

The two forces clashed, light against darkness, hope against despair. The air was filled with the sound of crackling energy, the ground trembling as the two powers battled for supremacy.

Eryndor could feel the strain, the darkness pressing in on them, threatening to overwhelm the light. But they knew that they could not give up, could not let the darkness win. They called upon the power of the Sword of Legends, channeling every ounce of strength they had into one final, desperate strike.

The sword blazed with a light that was brighter than the sun, a light that cut through the darkness like a beacon of hope. Eryndor swung the sword with all their might, the blade slicing through the air, cutting through the enemy's dark energy, and striking the leader with a force that shattered their armor and sent them crashing to the ground.

The leader let out a roar of agony, their body writhing as the light of the Sword of Legends seared through them. The dark energy that had fueled them began to dissipate, the flames around them flickering and dying as the light pushed back the darkness.

Eryndor stood over the fallen leader, their breath coming in ragged gasps. The battle was over, the enemy defeated. But the cost had been high, and the battlefield was littered with the bodies of the fallen.

The leader looked up at Eryndor, their eyes filled with a mixture of rage and fear. "You... you cannot stop the darkness. It is eternal..."

Eryndor shook their head, their voice filled with a quiet strength. "The darkness may be eternal, but so is the light. And as long as there are those who fight for it, the light will never be extinguished."

With a final, defiant snarl, the leader's body dissolved into shadows, the last remnants of their dark energy fading into the air. The battlefield grew quiet, the flames dying down, leaving only the aftermath of the battle.

Eryndor looked out over the plain, their heart heavy with the weight of the lives lost. The victory had come at a great cost, but it was a victory nonetheless. The enemy had been defeated, the darkness pushed back, and the light had prevailed.

As the allied forces began to regroup, tending to the wounded and honoring the fallen, Eryndor knew that the battle had been won, but the war was not over. The darkness would always be a threat, always lurking at the edges of the world, waiting for a chance to strike.

But as long as there were those who fought for the light, who believed in hope and justice, the darkness would never truly win.

The Battle of Blood and Fire had been fierce, but the light had emerged victorious.

And so, the Chosen One, with the Sword of Legends in hand, stood as a beacon of hope in a world that had been consumed by darkness. They knew that there would be more battles to come, more challenges to face. But they also knew that as long as they had the light, they could face whatever the future held.

The prophecy had been fulfilled, but the journey was far from over.

The light would continue to shine, and the battle for the future would go on.

End of Chapter 13

Chapter 14: The Sacrifice of the Fallen

The Aftermath of the Duel

The battlefield was a landscape of devastation. Smoke curled up from the charred earth, and the once-green plains had been turned into a wasteland of blood and ash. The cries of the wounded filled the air, mingling with the distant echoes of dying embers and the soft murmurs of the survivors. The final confrontation with the enemy's leader had left the allied forces in a fragile state—victorious, but at a cost so high it could scarcely be measured.

Eryndor stood amidst the ruins of the battlefield, the Sword of Legends still in their hand. The battle against the enemy's leader had drained them, both physically and emotionally. The power of the sword had saved them, had saved the allied forces, but it had come at the expense of their strength. Every muscle in their body ached, and a deep exhaustion had settled in their bones, an exhaustion that went beyond the physical.

Around them, the Fallen—Kael, Lyra, Torin, and Elara—were regrouping the remaining soldiers. Their faces were grim, their eyes hollowed by the weight of what they had seen and done. They were heroes, every one of them, and they had fought valiantly, but they too knew that the battle was not over. The enemy's forces had been decimated, but not completely destroyed. The remnants still gathered, still fought, still threatened to tip the balance of the war.

Eryndor approached their companions, their steps heavy but determined. They had come this far together, faced unimaginable horrors, and stood against the darkness as one. Now, in the final moments of the battle, they would need to dig deeper than ever before, to summon whatever strength they had left to finish what they had started.

Kael turned to Eryndor, his warhammer resting on his shoulder, a deep frown etched into his features. "It's not over yet, is it?"

Eryndor shook their head, their voice quiet but firm. "No. The leader is dead, but the enemy's forces still threaten us. They're regrouping for one last push. We can't let them succeed. If they break through our lines, everything we've fought for will be lost."

Lyra, ever the sharp-eyed warrior, scanned the battlefield, her expression unreadable. "We're running out of time. If we're going to stop them, we need to act now."

Torin, his fiery spirit undiminished despite the toll the battle had taken on him, nodded in agreement. "I can still muster enough magic to hold them off, but it won't last long. We need to strike hard and fast."

Elara, her gaze distant as she sought answers in the visions that had guided her for so long, spoke last. "The darkness is weakened, but it's not defeated. There's a chance—a slim one—but it will require sacrifice."

Eryndor looked at each of their companions in turn, their heart heavy with the knowledge of what needed to be done. The prophecy had always spoken of a great cost, of sacrifices that would need to be made to ensure victory. They had always known that this moment would come, but knowing it didn't make it any easier.

"We've come this far together," Eryndor said, their voice filled with resolve. "And I won't ask any of you to do anything I wouldn't do myself. But if we're going to end this, we need to be willing to make the ultimate sacrifice. For the light, for the future."

The Fallen were silent for a moment, each of them processing the gravity of the situation. They had fought for so long, had given so much, and now they were being asked to give everything. But they were warriors, each with their own reasons for fighting, their own tragedies that had shaped them into who they were. And in the end, they all knew that there was only one choice.

Kael was the first to speak, his deep voice steady and unyielding. "We've all lost something in this war. But we've also gained something—each other. If this is what it takes to protect what we've fought for, then I'm ready."

Lyra, her sharp eyes softened by a rare moment of vulnerability, nodded. "We've been through hell together. If this is the end, then at least we're facing it side by side."

Torin, ever the optimist, grinned despite the situation. "I've got one last trick up my sleeve. Let's make it count."

Elara, her voice calm and filled with a quiet strength, placed a hand on Eryndor's shoulder. "We were always meant to fight this battle, Eryndor. And we were always meant to do it together. Whatever happens, know that you're not alone."

Eryndor felt a surge of emotion, a mixture of pride, sorrow, and love for the companions who had become like family. They knew that the sacrifices they were about to make would be the hardest thing they had ever done, but they also knew that it was the only way to ensure victory.

"Thank you," Eryndor said, their voice filled with genuine gratitude. "Thank you for everything."

With that, the decision was made. The Fallen would make the ultimate sacrifice, giving their lives to protect the future of the world they had fought so hard to save. Their stories had come full circle, and now, in the final moments of the battle, they would cement their legacy as heroes.

The Final Stand

THE REMNANTS OF THE enemy's forces gathered on the far side of the battlefield, a mass of twisted creatures, dark sorcerers, and corrupted beasts. They were weakened, but they were not defeated. The death of their leader had left them disorganized, but the darkness that fueled them still burned strong, driving them to fight until the bitter end.

Eryndor and the Fallen led the remaining soldiers of the allied forces to the front lines, their presence a beacon of hope in the midst of the chaos. The soldiers, weary and bloodied from the battle, looked to them with a mixture of respect and desperation. They knew that this was it—the final push, the last stand against the darkness.

Eryndor raised the Sword of Legends high above their head, the blade glowing with a light that cut through the gloom. "This is our moment!" they shouted, their voice carrying over the battlefield. "For the light, for our future! We fight, we endure, and we prevail!"

A cheer rose up from the ranks of the allied forces, a sound filled with determination and resolve. The soldiers formed up in tight formations, their weapons ready, their hearts steeled for what was to come.

Kael, Lyra, Torin, and Elara took their positions at Eryndor's side, each of them ready to give everything they had for the cause they believed in. They knew that the odds were against them, but they also knew that they had something the enemy lacked—hope, courage, and the bonds that had been forged in the fires of battle.

The enemy surged forward, a tide of darkness that crashed against the allied lines with a ferocity born of desperation. The battle that followed was brutal, a chaotic melee of steel, magic, and blood. The ground beneath their feet became slick with the lifeblood of the fallen, the air thick with the stench of death and the roar of battle.

Kael fought with the strength of ten men, his warhammer smashing through the ranks of the enemy with relentless force. He was a wall of iron, unyielding and unstoppable, his presence a rallying point for the soldiers around him. But even Kael knew that he could not hold the line forever. The enemy's numbers were too great, their assault too fierce.

Lyra moved through the battlefield like a shadow, her twin daggers flashing as she struck down the dark sorcerers who sought to weaken the allied forces with their forbidden magic. She was a blur of motion, her movements graceful and deadly, but even she knew that her strength was waning. The enemy was relentless, their numbers seemingly endless, and Lyra could feel the weight of every strike, every cut, as it took its toll on her body.

Torin unleashed wave after wave of fire, his magic turning the battlefield into a blazing inferno. The flames roared and crackled, consuming everything in their path, but Torin knew that even fire had its limits. The enemy's dark sorcerers countered his magic with their own, and Torin could feel the strain of maintaining the inferno. His body ached, his magic flickering as he pushed himself to the brink.

Elara, her eyes filled with the knowledge of countless visions, guided the soldiers with a calm and steady hand. She anticipated the enemy's movements, directing the forces of light with precision and skill. But even Elara knew that her visions could only take them so far. The future was uncertain, and the enemy's determination was fierce. She could see the end coming, could feel the darkness closing in, but she refused to give in to despair.

Eryndor fought at the center of the allied forces, the Sword of Legends blazing with a light that pushed back the darkness. They struck down the enemy with every swing, their resolve unshaken despite the overwhelming odds. But even Eryndor knew that the situation was dire. The enemy was relentless, their numbers seemingly endless, and the allied forces were being pushed to their limits.

As the battle raged on, Eryndor realized that there was only one way to ensure victory, only one way to turn the tide in their favor. They turned to the Fallen, their heart heavy with the knowledge of what needed to be done.

"We need to end this now," Eryndor said, their voice filled with urgency. "If we don't, the enemy will overwhelm us. We need to take out their remaining leaders, cut the head off the snake."

Kael nodded, his expression grim but determined. "We can do it. We've faced worse odds before."

Lyra sheathed her daggers, her sharp eyes scanning the battlefield. "We'll need to move fast. They won't give us a second chance."

Torin grinned, despite the exhaustion etched into his features. "I've got enough fire left in me for one last show."

Elara's gaze was distant, her voice calm. "This is our moment. The future depends on what we do here."

Eryndor looked at each of their companions, their heart swelling with pride and sorrow. They knew that the sacrifices they were about to make would be the hardest thing they had ever done, but they also knew that it was the only way to ensure victory.

"Let's finish this," Eryndor said, their voice filled with resolve.

With that, the Fallen moved into position, each of them prepared to make the ultimate sacrifice. They knew that the battle would end here, one way or another, and they were determined to ensure that it ended in victory.

The Sacrifice

KAEL WAS THE FIRST to strike. He charged into the heart of the enemy's forces, his warhammer smashing through the ranks of the twisted creatures that stood in his way. He fought with a fury born of desperation, his strength unmatched as he tore through the enemy's lines. But even Kael knew that he could not hold the line forever. The enemy's forces were too vast, their power too great.

With a final, mighty swing of his warhammer, Kael shattered the ground beneath him, creating a massive chasm that cut through the enemy's ranks. The twisted creatures fell into the abyss, their screams echoing through the air as they were swallowed by the darkness.

But the effort took everything Kael had. His body, already battered and bruised from the battle, could not withstand the strain. With a final, defiant roar, Kael fell to his knees, his warhammer slipping from his grasp.

"Fight on," Kael murmured, his voice filled with a quiet strength. "Fight on for the light."

With that, Kael, the Unbroken, the warrior who had stood against the darkness with unwavering resolve, fell to the ground, his body still and lifeless.

Lyra was next. She moved through the battlefield like a shadow, her daggers flashing as she struck down the dark sorcerers who sought to weaken the allied forces with their forbidden magic. She was a blur of motion, her movements graceful and deadly, but even she knew that her strength was waning.

With a final burst of speed, Lyra reached the enemy's remaining leaders, the dark sorcerers who commanded the twisted creatures that still fought on the battlefield. She struck with deadly precision, her daggers finding their mark in the hearts of the sorcerers, cutting them down before they could unleash their dark magic.

But the effort took everything Lyra had. Her body, already weakened from the battle, could not withstand the strain. With a final, defiant breath, Lyra collapsed to the ground, her daggers slipping from her grasp.

"Let the light guide you," Lyra whispered, her voice filled with a quiet resolve. "Let the light guide you to victory."

With that, Lyra, the Shadowblade, the assassin who had fought in the shadows to protect the light, fell to the ground, her body still and lifeless.

Torin was next. He unleashed wave after wave of fire, his magic turning the battlefield into a blazing inferno. The flames roared and crackled, consuming everything in their path, but even Torin knew that his strength was fading.

With a final burst of energy, Torin unleashed a massive wave of fire, a wall of flames that swept across the battlefield, incinerating the enemy's remaining forces. The fire roared with a fury that seemed to consume the very air, the heat so intense that it could be felt even from a distance.

But the effort took everything Torin had. His body, already drained from the battle, could not withstand the strain. With a final, defiant grin, Torin collapsed to the ground, his hands still crackling with the remnants of his magic.

"Burn bright," Torin whispered, his voice filled with a quiet strength. "Burn bright for the light."

With that, Torin, the Flameborn, the mage who had fought with fire in his heart and fire in his hands, fell to the ground, his body still and lifeless.

Elara was the last. She guided the soldiers with a calm and steady hand, her visions allowing her to anticipate the enemy's movements and to direct the allied forces with precision. But even Elara knew that her strength was fading.

With a final burst of foresight, Elara guided the soldiers to the enemy's final stronghold, the last bastion of darkness on the battlefield. She directed the forces of light with a skill that was unmatched, her visions allowing her to see the enemy's every move before it happened.

But the effort took everything Elara had. Her mind, already strained from the countless visions she had seen, could not withstand the strain. With a final, defiant breath, Elara collapsed to the ground, her eyes closing as the visions faded.

"See the light," Elara whispered, her voice filled with a quiet strength. "See the light and follow it to victory."

With that, Elara, the Starseer, the seer who had guided the forces of light with her visions, fell to the ground, her body still and lifeless.

The Victory

THE SACRIFICES OF THE Fallen were not in vain. Their actions turned the tide of the battle, breaking the enemy's forces and giving the allied soldiers the strength and courage they needed to fight on. With the enemy's leaders defeated, the darkness that had fueled their forces began to fade, the twisted creatures crumbling to dust, the dark sorcerers falling where they stood.

Eryndor, their heart heavy with the loss of their companions, led the final charge, the Sword of Legends blazing with a light that cut through the last remnants of the darkness. The allied forces surged forward, their weapons raised high, their voices filled with the roar of victory.

The enemy's forces were shattered, their remnants scattered to the winds. The battle was over, the war won. But the cost had been great, and the battlefield was littered with the bodies of the fallen, their lifeblood soaking into the earth.

Eryndor stood at the center of the battlefield, their breath coming in ragged gasps, the Sword of Legends still in their hand. They looked out over the plain, their heart filled with a mixture of pride and sorrow. The victory had come at a terrible price, but it was a victory nonetheless.

The soldiers of the allied forces began to gather around Eryndor, their faces filled with a mixture of relief and grief. They had fought hard, had given everything they had, and now they stood victorious, but at the cost of so many lives.

Eryndor raised the Sword of Legends high above their head, the blade glowing with a light that cut through the gloom. "We have won!" they shouted, their voice carrying over the battlefield. "The darkness has been defeated! The light has prevailed!"

A cheer rose up from the ranks of the allied forces, a sound filled with hope, determination, and a fierce resolve. They had won, but they knew that the sacrifices they had made would never be forgotten.

As the soldiers began to tend to the wounded and to honor the fallen, Eryndor made their way to the bodies of their companions, their heart heavy with grief. Kael, Lyra, Torin, and Elara had given everything they had to protect the future of the world they loved, and now they lay still and silent, their bodies lifeless but their spirits unbroken.

Eryndor knelt beside their companions, their tears falling freely as they placed a hand on each of them in turn. "Thank you," they whispered, their voice filled with sorrow. "Thank you for everything. You will never be forgotten."

The sacrifices of the Fallen would be remembered as the turning point in the battle, the moment when the forces of light stood firm against the darkness and won. Their stories had come full circle, and their actions had inspired the remaining forces to fight with renewed vigor.

The light had prevailed, but it had come at a great cost.

The battle was over, but the memory of the Fallen would live on in the hearts of those who had fought beside them, in the songs that would be sung of their bravery, and in the future they had helped to protect.

Eryndor knew that the journey was far from over, that there would be more challenges to face, more battles to fight. But they also knew that the light would continue to shine, that the sacrifices of the Fallen had ensured a future worth fighting for.

And so, with the Sword of Legends in hand, Eryndor rose to their feet, their heart filled with a renewed sense of purpose. The battle was won, the darkness defeated, but the light would need to be protected, nurtured, and passed on to the generations to come.

The sacrifice of the Fallen had made it possible, and their legacy would live on.

END OF CHAPTER 14

Chapter 15: The Dawn of a New Era

The Quiet After the Storm

The battlefield that had been a scene of chaos, bloodshed, and fire was now eerily quiet. The smoke had begun to clear, revealing the scars that the war had left on the land—a once-vibrant plain now marred by craters, ashes, and the remnants of broken weapons. The sun, which had been obscured by the dark clouds of war, now broke through the haze, casting long rays of light over the desolate landscape.

Eryndor stood at the edge of what had once been the heart of the battle, the Sword of Legends held loosely in their hand. The blade, which had burned so brightly with the light of hope, now shimmered softly, its duty fulfilled. The war was over, the darkness defeated, and the prophecy fulfilled. But as the light of dawn illuminated the scene before them, Eryndor could not help but feel the weight of the loss that had brought them to this moment.

Around them, the survivors of the allied forces moved slowly, tending to the wounded, gathering the bodies of the fallen, and beginning the long, painful task of rebuilding. The victory had come at a great cost, and the faces of those who had lived to see it were etched with exhaustion, sorrow, and a deep sense of relief. The battle was over, but the work of healing had only just begun.

Eryndor looked out over the battlefield, their heart heavy with the memories of those who had fought beside them, those who had made the ultimate sacrifice. The Fallen—Kael, Lyra, Torin, and Elara—were gone, their lives given to protect the future of the world they loved. Their absence was a void that Eryndor felt keenly, a reminder of the cost of the war and the burden of leadership.

As the sun continued to rise, casting its golden light over the land, Eryndor knew that a new era was dawning. The war was over, the darkness pushed back, but the future that lay ahead was uncertain. The world had been forever changed by the conflict, and the task of rebuilding it, of leading the kingdoms into an era of peace, would be the greatest challenge yet.

The Rebuilding Begins

THE ALLIED FORCES HAD been reduced to a fraction of their original strength, but their spirit remained unbroken. The leaders of the surviving kingdoms gathered in the Sacred Grove, the place where the alliance had been forged, to discuss the future. The grove, once a sanctuary of peace, now bore the marks of war, but it was still a place of power, a place where the light of hope could be rekindled.

King Aldric of Thaloria, his once-proud armor dented and bloodstained, spoke first. "We have won a great victory," he said, his voice steady but weary. "But it has come at a terrible cost. Our lands are scarred, our people devastated. We must rebuild, and we must do so together."

King Aerandir of Valandor, his silver hair now streaked with ash, nodded in agreement. "The war has shown us the strength of unity. The elves of Valandor will do everything in our power to help restore what has been lost. The balance of the world must be restored, and that will require all of us."

King Thrain of Stonehelm, his gruff voice softened by the weight of the losses his people had suffered, added, "Stonehelm will lend its strength to the rebuilding effort. Our forges will burn bright, not for weapons of war, but for tools of peace."

Eryndor listened to the leaders of the kingdoms, their heart swelling with a mixture of pride and sorrow. The war had forced them to come together, to set aside their differences and fight for a common cause. But now that the war was over, the challenge would be to maintain that unity, to build a future where peace could endure.

"We have been through much," Eryndor said, stepping forward to address the gathered leaders. "The war has taken a toll on all of us, and the road ahead will not be easy. But we have also proven that when we stand together, we are capable of overcoming even the darkest of threats. The prophecy has been fulfilled, but our work is far from over. We must rebuild our world, and we must do so with the same determination and unity that saw us through the war."

The leaders nodded in agreement, their expressions serious but hopeful. The task ahead was daunting, but they were ready to face it together. The scars of the war would take time to heal, but with cooperation and trust, they could begin to restore what had been lost.

Over the following weeks, the leaders of the kingdoms worked tirelessly to coordinate the rebuilding efforts. The ruins of the cities and villages that had been destroyed were cleared, and new foundations were laid. The forests that had been burned were replanted, and the rivers that had run red with blood began to flow clear once more.

The elves of Valandor used their magic to heal the land, restoring the natural balance that had been disrupted by the war. The dwarves of Stonehelm lent their craftsmanship to the construction of new buildings and fortifications, ensuring that the structures would stand the test of time. The soldiers of Thaloria, who had fought so bravely on the battlefield, now turned their efforts to rebuilding their homeland, their swords and shields replaced by tools and shovels.

Eryndor traveled from kingdom to kingdom, lending their support and guidance wherever it was needed. They met with the leaders, the soldiers, and the common people, listening to their concerns and offering words of encouragement. They knew that the process of rebuilding would take time, but they also knew that it was the only way to ensure a lasting peace.

As the days turned into weeks, and the weeks into months, the world slowly began to heal. The scars of the war would never be fully erased, but the people of the kingdoms were determined to move forward, to build a future where such a conflict would never happen again.

The Challenge of Leadership

WITH THE REBUILDING well underway, Eryndor found themselves facing a new challenge: leading the kingdoms into an era of peace. The war had united them in a common cause, but now that the threat of the darkness had been vanquished, old rivalries and tensions began to resurface. The leaders of the kingdoms, who had fought side by side on the battlefield, now found themselves grappling with the complexities of governance, with the need to balance the interests of their people with the greater good of the world.

Eryndor knew that maintaining the unity that had been forged in the crucible of war would be no easy task. The kingdoms were diverse, each with its own customs, traditions, and priorities. But they also knew that the lessons of the war could not be forgotten, that the peace they had fought so hard to achieve could not be taken for granted.

To address these challenges, Eryndor called for a council of leaders to be held in the Sacred Grove, the same place where the alliance had been formed. The council would be a place for dialogue, for the resolution of disputes, and for the coordination of efforts to maintain peace and stability in the world.

The leaders of the kingdoms responded to Eryndor's call, gathering once again in the Sacred Grove. The atmosphere was different from the days of the war—there was no longer the pressing urgency of survival, but there was a recognition of the importance of the task at hand.

"Peace is a fragile thing," Eryndor said as they addressed the council. "It requires constant effort, constant vigilance. We have won the war, but the peace we have achieved is only the beginning. We must work together to ensure that it endures."

King Aldric, who had always been a staunch advocate for Thaloria's independence, spoke up. "I agree, Eryndor, but we must also ensure that each kingdom retains its sovereignty. We cannot allow the alliance to become a means of imposing the will of one kingdom over another."

King Aerandir nodded in agreement. "The elves of Valandor value our independence as much as any other kingdom. But we also recognize that the world is interconnected. What happens in one kingdom can have far-reaching consequences for the others. We must find a way to balance our independence with our collective responsibility."

King Thrain, ever the pragmatist, added, "Stonehelm will always stand by its allies, but we must also ensure that our people's needs are met. We cannot neglect our own in the pursuit of a greater good."

Eryndor listened to the concerns of the leaders, understanding the delicate balance that needed to be struck. The unity that had been forged in war could not be maintained through force or coercion; it had to be based on mutual respect, on the recognition of the importance of both independence and cooperation.

"We must find a way to work together while respecting each kingdom's sovereignty," Eryndor said. "The council we establish here today will be a place where we can discuss our differences, resolve disputes, and coordinate our efforts for the greater good. It will be a place where every kingdom's voice is heard, where decisions are made collectively, not imposed from above."

The leaders considered Eryndor's proposal, their expressions thoughtful. They knew that the success of the council would depend on their willingness to engage in dialogue, to compromise when necessary, and to prioritize the long-term stability of the world over short-term gains.

After much discussion, the leaders agreed to establish the council, with Eryndor as its first chair. The council would meet regularly in the Sacred Grove, and its decisions would be based on consensus, with each kingdom having an equal say in the matters that were brought before it.

The establishment of the council was a significant step forward, a recognition of the need for a new way of governing in a world that had been forever changed by the war. It was a challenge, to be sure, but it was also an opportunity—a chance to build a future where peace could endure, where the mistakes of the past would not be repeated.

Reflection on the Cost of War

AS THE DAYS PASSED, and the work of rebuilding continued, Eryndor found themselves reflecting on the cost of the war. The victory had been hard-won, but it had come at a terrible price. The lives that had been lost, the cities and villages that had been destroyed, the scars that had been left on the land and on the hearts of the people—these were the legacies of the conflict, reminders of the darkness that had threatened to consume the world.

Eryndor often visited the graves of the Fallen, where Kael, Lyra, Torin, and Elara had been laid to rest. Their final resting place was in a quiet corner of the Sacred Grove, beneath the ancient trees that had witnessed so much of the world's history. The graves were marked with simple stones, each inscribed with the name of the one who lay beneath it.

Kael the Unbroken, who had stood as a bastion of strength and resilience.

Lyra the Shadowblade, who had fought with grace and deadly precision in the shadows.

Torin the Flameborn, who had wielded the power of fire with unmatched skill and passion.

Elara the Starseer, who had guided the forces of light with her visions and wisdom.

Eryndor knelt before the graves, their heart heavy with the weight of the losses they had suffered. The Fallen had given everything to protect the future of the world they loved, and their sacrifices had made the victory possible. But their absence was a void that could never be filled, a reminder of the cost of the war.

"I miss you," Eryndor whispered, their voice filled with sorrow. "I wish you were here to see what we're building. I wish you were here to help guide us into this new era. But I know that you gave your lives for this—for the chance to build a better world, a world where the light can shine without fear of the darkness."

As they spoke, Eryndor felt a sense of peace, a quiet reassurance that the Fallen had not died in vain. Their legacy would live on in the world they had helped to protect, in the hearts of the people who had fought beside them, and in the future that was now being built.

The cost of the war had been great, but it had also given the world a chance to start anew. The scars would remain, but they would be a reminder of the resilience of the human spirit, of the strength that could be found in unity, and of the hope that could endure even in the darkest of times.

The Hope for a Brighter Future

AS THE MONTHS TURNED into years, the world slowly began to heal. The scars of the war, both physical and emotional, would never fully fade, but the people of the kingdoms were determined to move forward. The council established by Eryndor became a place of dialogue and cooperation, a symbol of the unity that had been forged in the crucible of war.

The rebuilding efforts continued, and the world began to flourish once more. The cities that had been destroyed were rebuilt, stronger and more resilient than before. The forests that had been burned were replanted, their trees growing tall and strong. The rivers that had run red with blood now flowed clear and pure, a symbol of the renewal that was taking place.

The people of the kingdoms, who had once been divided by old rivalries and tensions, now found common ground in their shared experiences. The war had shown them the importance of unity, and they were determined to maintain the peace that had been so hard-won. The lessons of the past were not forgotten, but they were used to build a better future, a future where peace could endure.

Eryndor continued to lead the council, guiding the kingdoms with wisdom and compassion. They knew that the challenges of leadership were many, and that the road ahead would not always be smooth, but they were committed to the task. They had fulfilled their destiny as the Chosen One, but they also knew that their work was not done. The dawn of a new era had come, and it was up to them to ensure that it was a bright and hopeful one.

As they looked out over the world they had helped to rebuild, Eryndor felt a deep sense of satisfaction, a quiet joy in knowing that the sacrifices that had been made had not been in vain. The light had prevailed, and the world had been given a second chance.

The future was still uncertain, but it was also filled with possibility. The people of the kingdoms had shown that they were capable of great things when they stood together, and Eryndor had faith that they would continue to build on the foundation that had been laid.

The dawn of a new era had arrived, and with it came the hope for a brighter future.

As the sun set on the world that had been forever changed by the war, Eryndor knew that the journey was far from over. There would be more challenges to face, more battles to fight, but they also knew that the light would continue to shine, that hope would continue to endure.

And as long as there was hope, there was a future worth fighting for.

End of Chapter 15

End of Book

Did you love *The Blood of the Fallen*? Then you should read *The Forgotten City*[1] by Patrick William Lee!

The Forgotten City is a captivating journey through a world of ancient prophecies, mystical trials, and the rebirth of a lost civilization. Follow Elara, a young villager marked by destiny, as she uncovers the secrets of a forgotten city hidden deep within the mountains. Through trials of wit, courage, and inner strength, she confronts the city's dark curse and awakens its timeless wisdom. A tale of discovery, redemption, and the enduring legacy of knowledge, this story will inspire generations to come.

---

1. https://books2read.com/u/3nPZWo

2. https://books2read.com/u/3nPZWo

About the Author

Patrick William Lee is a renowned author celebrated for his enchanting tales of magic and wonder. Specializing in the genres of fairy tales, folk tales, legends, and mythology, Patrick weaves stories that transport readers to fantastical realms where the impossible becomes reality. With a deep love for folklore and a talent for crafting timeless narratives, his books captivate the imaginations of readers young and old. When he's not writing, Patrick enjoys exploring ancient forests, studying mythical creatures, and sharing his passion for storytelling with audiences around the world. His works continue to inspire and delight, leaving a lasting impact on the world of literature.